Jean McNeil was born in 1968 and grew up on Cape Breton island in Canada but has lived in London since 1991. *Hunting Down Home,* her first novel, was published in 1996; she is also the author of the *Rough Guide to Costa Rica* and a contributor to the *Rough Guide to Central America.* She works as an editor and researcher at the Latin American Bureau in London.

By Jean McNeil

Hunting Down Home
Nights in a Foreign Country

Hunting Down Home

JEAN McNEIL

PHŒNIX

A PHOENIX PAPERBACK

First published in Great Britain
by Phoenix House in 1996
This paperback edition published in 1997
by Phoenix, a division of Orion Books Ltd,
Orion House, 5 Upper St Martin's Lane,
London WC2H 9EA

Second impression 2001

A CIP catalogue record for this book is available
from the British Library.

ISBN: 1 85799 870 7

Printed and bound in Great Britain by
The Guernsey Press Co. Ltd,
Guernsey, Channel Islands

This book is for
C. A. MacDonald (1921–1989) and J. C. McNeil (1919–1990)
of Boularderie Island, Cape Breton, Nova Scotia

THANKS

I feel a great debt to those who have made it possible for this book to be published: to my agent, Jane Bradish-Ellames of Curtis Brown UK, who has worked so hard on my behalf; to my editor, Maggie McKernan, and to Alison Walsh, both of Phoenix House in London; to Louise Dennys and Susan Burns in Toronto for reading an earlier draft of this work; to Linda Taylor, for her advice and for giving me the space to work in London. To Janet McNeil for, amongst other things, her transformational images of southern Africa, among the best examples of photography I have ever seen. Above all I want to thank Nick Dennys, without whose friendship and support I would not have been able to write this, or any other, book.

SWIMMING
TO AFRICA

I THINK of her all the time now that I am the age she was when she disappeared. I have dreams of swimming to Africa to rescue her.

Ahead of me are the burning shores of the Gambia, or Ethiopia, or Namibia. Their butter-soft syllables roll off the tongue smoothly only to disintegrate in the noon-struck heat. On the shore the sand is washed to silver by the sea. The thick-leaved livid plants rasp in their continual photosynthesis.

Storms come in the afternoon, fierce rainstorms – the kind only the tropics can brew. The clouds clamp a giant lid down on the broiling pot of land and light, gas-blue, leaks from around its rim.

We both wake glutted by humidity into these seasonal rains. I live in the tropics, on the same latitude, the tropic of Capricorn. I can almost smell her; she smells like negative ions cracked open by lightning. Each of us knows the other is out there. We can finger the slight depressions made by the impact of our bodies on one another. How I ransacked her in my mindless organisms' insistence upon mitosis. How she formed my fingers.

When she looks out of her window she sees the clouds clearing away, racing toward the Indian Ocean; a few slanted rays of sunlight hounding them from the west. Children play in the garden, laughing in the same staccato language as splashes made in puddles. She traces the flow of the rivulets of rain running down her windows with her fingertip; that fingertip which has the same conformation as mine. In their liquid frames the kwashiorkor victim palms warp and spindle. She presses her head against the cool of the window just as a fresh sheet of rain hits the glass.

Then we are at Lake Nyasa at dawn. This is not my memory, but an image reflected in the shards of a mirror dropped by someone who has gone ahead of me. She and her friend Margaret have hitchhiked back from Dar es Salaam and have come upon the lake in the morning. The fishermen cast their nets among spindle-legged flamingos and white ibis. Water buffalo break the surface like submarines.

Behind them now is Dar es Salaam, that slum-in-progress where Africa and Asia Minor meet, and Oyster Bay's phosphorus sands. Offshore communist bloc supertankers bleed rust into the hot carbonized water of the Indian ocean.

Wafting behind them too are the men in long robes, the hems of which brush the southern fingertips of Islam. Their daisy-cutting gait is a reminder of the days when the languorous fingers of the Arab traders were so deeply spiced in the smells of Zanzibar's cloves they had long since turned dark brown. These were the same cloves that would end up in the basement depths of ships to be taken to the north for Christmas, when they would be stuck in oranges, searing the delicate, once-inviolate flesh with their chemical stings.

These were the same cloves that would stain the fingers of Christine, Bridget's mother, my grandmother, as she made the Christmas cake that last year.

SUMMER

ONE

T̲HE kitchen was a lung cancer sauna. Smoke from the three lit cigarettes mingled with the fuggy heat.

'Sure as I'm sitting here, that's what he did.' She turned to her two sisters, who flanked her on either side like a crumpled Imperial guard. ' "You've got to get help," I says. "Will you ever act your age, man?" I says. I feel sorry for him.' She shook her head. 'But you either shit or get off the pot. And he's still sitting there.'

'Waiting for you to come and wipe his arse,' her sister Jessie said.

In her rocking chair my grandmother shrugged, and an ash dropped from her cigarette. 'I don't know. He's never really known himself. He's just twisted himself into shapes. Who can blame him, with what he has for a mother?'

'Never you mind, Christine,' her sister Maryanne counselled. 'It's just some kind of crisis. It's a private thing between himself and himself. It has nothing to do with you.'

The squeaking of the rocking chair punctuated their conversation. My grandmother took another drag on her cigarette.

'He knows very well she's coming back,' she said, suddenly fierce. 'He's known that since last fall. I told him myself. He knows Morag will go with her. Why shouldn't she?' she appealed to her sisters, stabbing her cigarette in their direction.

Jessie nodded. 'But he has to put on a big production, as usual.'

'I've given him a lot of latitude – ' my grandmother sat back in her chair ' – and he knows it too.'

'Well, he's been all over the world, up and down,' Maryanne snorted. 'He's been to the Equator, so he must be better than us, right? Doesn't that just figure. He knows things we can't know just by sitting on our arses here in Cape Breton.'

Their talk of men was always like this: bewilderment and reprimand mixed with an equal measure of contempt. Like they talked about children. Like they talked about me.

Every evening when I was supposed to be in bed I was in fact upstairs, poised over the register, the iron-covered hole in the ceiling which allowed the stove's heat to rise to the second floor. Hung upside down like a bat, my heart in my mouth, my ear a minute steak braising on the hot grille. I overheard entire conversations in this position. No one guessed why I was prone to earaches. Ever since I could remember, I had had to resort to the tactics of creatures who are simultaneously witness, spy and pawn.

'I don't know. It's not the drink any more.' My grandmother's voice drifted up through the ceiling. 'I think it's his mind.'

They were silent for a while. Rum glasses were placed on the kitchen table with tiny raps.

Jessie snorted. 'The situation he left you in. I've never seen the likes of it. What a bastard. If it were me, I'd never forgive him for what he did.'

'Well it's not you, is it?' My grandmother rocked the chair back and forth on the balls of her feet. I could see her face in between the slats of the register. Her lips were set; she looked pleased, as if surveying her work.

'Well, I don't know.' Maryanne fingered her rum glass. 'We're not in your position. But I'm inclined to agree. We may have known him all our lives. But he's still a bastard.'

Which was what they sometimes called me, too.

That summer was the hottest anyone could remember. It brought a quick-fire, scorching heat between eleven in the morning and three in the afternoon, which then faded desultorily into the mauve evening. At times we thought a southern current or a sirocco had drifted wildly off course and had slammed into the north Atlantic by mistake. The nights were alchemical, as if there was some transformative element at work. The traditional kitchen parties were moved outside to fields, or to the night-glittering shore where we built bonfires and went swimming in a water so warm that it was indistinguishable from the air, and so black we might have been swimming through melted chocolate or licorice, some sweet thick substance without boundaries or end.

For the field parties we arrived in trucks and parked at the top of the cliffs on the South Side, overlooking the water. Fifteen or sixteen trucks and cars would congregate at the cliffs or at the beach, headlights cutting the night in front of them like the eyes of saurian monsters. Racoons and bears scuttled out of the way of our nocturnal onslaught. We spread plaid blankets in the back of the flatbeds, once all the hay had been swept out. Ham sandwiches and beer were laid out, radios were tuned to CBC in Sydney, and headlights were left on, illuminating a space of grass that doubled as a dance floor. Sometimes my grandfather tuned up and we had a dance right there in the middle of the field, the dry grass tickling our calves.

They drank prodigiously into the humid night. We kids lay on our backs and watched the stars gather about our heads. We would be found there, four or five hours later, fast asleep, separated and delicately placed into our respective trucks and station wagons and driven home into the blinding promise of another scorching morning.

'Let's go in, Morag.'

We stood knee-deep in felled grass listening to the crows' caws fill the empty evening as we tied rough string on the last bales of hay with our calloused hands. The bales of hay trailed behind us like corpses on a battlefield. The light disappeared over the cusp of the horizon.

My grandfather and I had been haying for most of August. The grass was ready about two weeks earlier than usual, and we worked all day in the blinding heat. We had dealt with scores of stinging hay bales, decapitated the snakes, squashed the beetles and weevils. Our skin was covered in mosquito- and hay-bitten red welts, which looked like scar tissue and required sloppy doses of pink calamine lotion to be applied late at night, when the sun had finally sunk.

We heard a yelp and thought it was the dog, until we saw her come sailing out of the Big House in the distance, holding the screen door open with one hand and waving furiously with the other.

'Ignore her. She's just itching to eat supper.'

'I'm itching, too,' I complained, scratching my chest.

'Finish that bale, and then we can go.' He chewed a blade of grass, and pushed his battered leather fedora – veteran of many salt-cold Atlantic crossings as well as the scorching sun of Sicily – back on his head. He looked full into the last orange flares of the setting sun, and his face caught the blue reflection of the mountain, which in turn had caught the violet hue of the lake between our field and the creased ancient Appalacian hills.

My grandfather looked like Hitler, there was no denying it. He was not nearly as ugly, but he had the same small square black moustache and dark hair brushed to the side. Still only in his late forties, he remained at the height of his physical powers. Small and wiry, like a twisted coathanger, with a slightly hooked nose and a perpetually mean expression. With his rigid intensity he had the manner of a trapped animal about to spring out of your hand once you think you have caught it. He had been a featherweight boxing champion in his youth, and years of shovelling coal into the burners of Norwegian merchant marine ships and the huge barges that plied the shores of the Great Lakes in the thirties had given him arms whose muscles knotted like a ship's ropes.

He sighed, waiting for her to stop gesticulating. He took off his hat and wiped his brow, and shouted in a guttural, hay-musted voice.

'Hold your horses.'

Hor ... es, hor ... es. The echo filled the empty evening like cold water poured into a glass. My throat burned with hay-dust and heat.

And then we saw her coming toward us. She was running, apron bouncing ahead of her churning legs, over the hayfield.

'What in the name of Jesus ...' he began. We had never seen her run before. In her long, loping ascent of the last field she came on like a Masai warrior drifting across the salt-bed of an evaporated lake.

She reached us, and stood breathless.

'She's coming,' she breathed, rather than said. All her limbs were trembling. The sturdy shoes she wore were covered in hay-dust.

My grandfather stopped chewing his grass.

'She's coming,' she repeated, her voice rising. 'In the spring.'

The crickets started to hum in the ditch beside the fence. A mosquito bit me, and I scratched where the hay had cut my skin. I caught the mosquito between my finger and thumb and crushed it. My own blood spilled out from its body and stained my palm.

'Jesus,' he breathed. 'Are you sure?'

Why were they behaving so strangely? I wanted to go inside, away from the stinging bites of the mosquitoes and the blackflies. I yawned and scratched. I put my arms around myself: it was cooling off already.

I asked, 'Who?'

'You've even got hay down your front.' She pulled my T-shirt off. By then I had nearly fallen asleep on my feet and needed only a gentle push onto the bed.

'I thought only horses slept on their feet,' she laughed, before scraping away the sweaty strands of hay which had given me blotchy bumps on the paint-white chest where my breasts would one day grow.

And then I fell into the deep trough of night.

I came down in the morning to find them squaring off against each other.

'What's going on?'

'Never you mind,' she turned to me. 'I'm just asking your grandfather to explain something to me, once and for all.' She stood with her arms folded. She had seen the scythe leaning against the wall in the porch. 'I'm going to ask you again,' she told him, 'because I want to know. What's that on the scythe, Sandy?' She pointed accusingly to it.

'No.' He shook his head. He wanted to forget about it.

'The brown on the blade – I know it's blood.' She peered at it more closely. 'What did you kill? I have to go out in those fields too. I have every right to know.'

He had seen that snake, a four-foot-long black cord swimming through the hay, a second before cutting it neatly in two. Its separate halves had squirmed grotesquely as if trying to meld again and go off in some singular direction, and then were still.

He never told her how big the snakes were. As far as I knew he wasn't afraid of anything, but he would shiver after these decapitations. Our land was swampy, with one of the fields separated by a heat-absorbing stone wall where snakes liked to breed and sun themselves as they grew to an unnaturally large size. That night he had nightmares that the snake was inside his head. He could see its tail poking out of his right ear, a black eel squirming on his pillow. I know, because we swapped accounts of our respective snake nightmares at breakfast every morning.

The strawberries were long gone with the departure of the livid days of June. The stolid beets, the thin quivering carrots and the green peas had been pulled from the ground, which had held tenaciously onto their root fingers. The rhubarb patch at the back of the house had already flowered in its tropical, sinister manner; its edible stems ruffed by poisonous leaves. The spindly apple tree, silver with age, began to yield its annual five crates of windfalls a month earlier than usual.

Everything seemed to be happening too fast. The clouds raced across the sky in a hurry, as if being sucked out to sea. Grandma found her first grey hairs, even though she was only forty-five. Plums parachuted from the trees by the brook. All our fruit was ripening and rotting before we could get it into the shed, into the cellar, into the pickling jars that kept us going through the winter.

We stood outside watching the sun go down behind the black face of the mountain.

'It's against nature.' He held his hand flat over his brow, squinting into the Bras d'or lakes, now gold and plated with evening.

'It's the end of the world,' she said.

Then they laughed and each cracked open a beer. I listened to the liquid gurgle down their hot throats; it was the same sound I heard when we went to fetch the fresh-shot deer carcasses, hauling them up off the ground, still warm, as blood bubbled up their gullets.

These are the coordinates: 46°N, 60.30°W. This is the oldest part of the country, in terms of its recorded history. We were discovered more or less first. We are the first landfall on the long arcing sea route from the bony-fingered island homes of the great navigating kingdoms, just as these days Goose Bay on the northeast tip of Labrador is the first landfall for the jets that commute the North Atlantic corridor.

Prince Henry Sinclair, Navigator, Adventurer and Laird of the Orkney Islands found it in 1398, closely followed or preceded (they left no traces, being interested only in offshore plunder) by Portuguese fishermen. Vikings had probably been there first, but unlike Newfoundland no rib-caged longboat wrecks have ever mushroomed overnight on our shores, blooming from the sifting sands.

The island is a dying place that will never die, like Carthage smouldering for centuries in the Romans' wake. We have been ransacked as efficiently as if we had been visited by the Mongol hordes, floating on their tiny horses, sailing above the steppes like a giant hovercraft. But the island will survive because it is so remote it could be Samarkand – the waterless land where turquoise friezes stretch their lithe muscles into the equally turquoise sky. On a map of Nova Scotia it is the ungainly shape at the top, like an encephalitic head balanced on a bony body. It does not even look like an island. One mile of water is all that separates it from the mainland. But that one mile wide is also one mile deep, among the deepest guts in the Atlantic. It is formed by a trough in the North American continental shelf, a seam so deep that even when they had blasted away half a mountain to build the Causeway, they could not fill it.

'See that cloud?' he pointed, squinting against the sun into a jagged-fingered cloud anchored in the sky. 'That's what Scotland looks like.' France was there, too, its huge bulk drifting over the west coast of the island, settling over Cheticamp and disgorging its cargo of emigrants like rain. The Micmac called it *Wunama'kik*: 'foggy land', where clouds and mists the colour of the white man's skin foamed up from the sea like boiled milk.

The names speak of no good portent, of a place metallic and pre-destroyed: *Black Brook. Ironville. Wreck Cove. Blues Mills. Reserve Mines. North Gut.*

We had come here from barren islands on creaky ships. Strange birds cried at night, and came to nest on the riggings when the sea was calm. And as we neared land we could smell it before the skipper could, because we were people of the sea and knew the thick, putrid and fertile smell of land.

'Smells like a cunt.'

'Well,' my grandfather shrugged, and lit his cigarette. 'That's what I would have said.'

The North: our mountain–scraped sea, the wolf's eye, molecules of dead navigators smashed on the rocks.

I have nightmares every night. I am seven years old.

TWO

H<small>E</small> threw the postcard down on the kitchen table. On the front was the double scene of an elephant and a giant waterfall.

'Maybe I'm losing my grip on the English language.' He scratched his head. 'But I can't make head nor tail of this.'

My grandmother put on her reading glasses and creased her brow in anticipation of the coming understanding. After she had read it, she put the card down and took off her glasses, staring out the kitchen window, past the silver-limbed apple tree, into the blue of the water and the distance.

When they had both gone away I tried out my reading.

'I am here in Nigeria, we drove by a smoking Landrover, all around which lay bodies or what looked like bodies, because here you cannot tell a burnt-out axle from a burnt-out man.'

No name, no more. That was all it said.

'Well,' she sighed, putting her glasses back on the table, where they still retained the shape and warmth of her head. 'I've been saving up some slides she sent that came last week. Why don't we have a little show tonight?'

'My God, them baboons.' She drew in her breath sharply. 'Shameless, aren't they?'

Bridget had a family of baboons in her back yard, most of

them indecorous, thrusting their mis-named private parts into the camera's lens.

The thick haying gloves had been cast on the floor. My grandfather sat wearing only a singlet and his shorts, a bottle of beer cooling the hot flesh on the inside of his thighs. Sweat ran down the deep ravine between my grandmother's breasts underneath her sleeveless polyester shirt. The refrigerator hummed, disproportionately loud, the only sound besides the clack-clacking of the projector as the slides were changed.

The women in the images walked like thoroughbreds; their pace slow, voluptuous, stately. We could see this even in the freeze-frame universe of the expanded photographs.

My grandparents said little. They never offered any explanation as to why these stark images flitted across our walls the way that television's blue light flickered through other houses' rooms. The refrigerator and the projector would hum in turn and we could hear the brook's slippery breath as it ran alongside the house.

In the evenings they listened to the international news on the radio, the reports that came tripping out of the box all the way from Toronto or Vancouver, the reports that mentioned places that all sounded the same, names like Zimbabwe, Zambia, Botswana or Namibia; the melodious country names mentioned in conjunction with fascist-sounding acronyms – ZANLA, SWAPO, FRELIMO, UNITA, Idi Amin...

Sometimes after listening to these reports her face would be pleated with worry.

'I'm afeard for her. Let's sit down and say a rosary.' She thrust the wine-coloured beads into my hands, reached into her pocket and extracted her reserve set. We sat down at the kitchen table, the vinyl sticking to my hot legs, and began murmuring.

'Ourfatherwhoardineavenallowedbethynamethykingdomcome thywillbedoneonearthasitisineaven.' I didn't really know the words: I just made the sounds. We continued our murmuring, until I fell asleep somewhere around 'blessed are the fruit of thy womb, Jesus'. I had no idea what a womb might be, but I drifted off thinking of fruit; of the late summer plums and their delirious sweetness and of the sour bite of autumn's first apples.

He flicked his eyes from mirror to mirror, on the lookout for the RCMP as we roared through the outskirts of the city. He drove with his knees, using one hand to light a cigarette and the other to swig from a forty-ouncer of rum which he held tight between his thighs. We passed the K-Mart while Cutlass Supremes whizzed by, low-slung like revolvers or penile projectiles filled with men who owned eight-track cassette players and green felt dice swinging from the rear-view mirror.

We were heading home on the Trans-Canada Highway in whatever doomed car he owned at the time – in those days his cars had a prognosis of about six months followed by a quick, violent death. He had been playing at a summer concert and the trunk was packed with his amps, his guitars and harmonicas and fiddles. He was humming a tune and beating out a rhythm on the steering wheel with his palms.

We passed the Lick-a-Chick, dressed up in pink and orange neon, tantalizing us from the highway. Sometimes we would stop here on our way back from a party, usually about one or two in the morning, so that he could soak up some alcohol with the greasy breaded chicken they served all night. I always woke up to accompany him inside. It was a different world in there – done up like a second-rate Kentucky Fried Chicken, with white-varnished plywood and lurid cafeteria heatlamps and young girls with spotty faces from standing over the grill. Then he drove the rest of the way home eating the chicken, which he kept on his lap. From time to time took a drink from the forty-ouncer, often at the same time as lighting his cigarette. Because his hands were fully occupied at these moments he would drive with his knees. We spent a lot of time in ditches, but he usually did that on purpose. Otherwise his knees had excellent reflexes.

Suddenly, he swerved.

'Holy shit.' He looked over his shoulder. 'It's him.'

'Go away with you,' she dismissed him from her position in the passenger seat. All the same she looked sideways at the truck we were passing.

I looked over, too, from the back seat, where I sat with my binoculars on my lap. I used them for spotting licence plates – Florida's pink flamingo, Saskatchewan's puff of amber wheat. I raised the binoculars to my eyes.

In the truck was a family, or at least what looked like a family. They were so close, magnified in the lens, that I could have been in the truck right beside them. A man at the steering wheel, a tired looking blonde woman, and two smudged-faced kids in the back seat of the cab. The man and the woman were oblivious to the three people in the car passing them, ogling and pointing; they didn't even see the binoculars. The kids noticed, though, and we exchanged blank looks just as I brought the binoculars down.

She sucked in her breath.

'My God,' she breathed. 'It is him. Who's that he's got with him?'

'Dunno. His wife I guess. Looks like they got kids.'

'Well,' she snorted, 'I hope he's good and happy.'

I looked at them again. We were just about past, our back bumper edging out over their front hood. I swivelled around. The man looked harassed. The woman was leaning over to do something – change the radio station, probably. The kids plunged their fingers into open potato chip bags and excavated greasy crumbs.

'What are you talking about?' I stuck my head forward into the front seat.

'Never you mind,' he growled. He put his elbow into my nose and shoved me backwards.

'You gave me a nosebleed,' I wailed, watching the blood spatter onto my knees.

She whipped around with the Kleenex, thrusting the tissue at me.

'You just keep quiet,' she commanded.

In the front seat I heard him mumble something. All I caught was the word 'father'.

'What're you talking about?' I poked my face back in between the front bucket seats again. 'What's a father?'

My grandmother rolled her eyes. 'Where'd you leave your brains? Timbuktu? What do you mean "what's a father". Everybody's got a father. Now get back there.' She pushed me back.

'Is he my father,' I asked, looking at Grandpa.

'He is not,' she snapped. 'He's your grandfather. You know that.'

'Well then, I don't have a father,' I reasoned, tilting my nose back to the roof again.

'Yes, you do. That was him in the pickup truck we just passed.'

My grandfather gave me a savage look in the rear-view mirror. 'Now will you mind your own business?'

'Why're you picking on me?' I wailed. 'You're the one who talked to me.'

'Do you want me to drive us all off the road?'

I'd been off the road with him enough times. I slumped and shut up.

'Father' really meant nothing to me. It was as if she had said, 'That was your rhinoceros we just passed in that pickup truck.' So I forgot about the whole thing a couple of miles down the road, the white meridians flashing under our wheels like bones, measuring the distance home.

'Where the hell are you going?' She stood over him with her hands fixed in the hollow between her waist and her hip.

'Out with my goddamn friends.' He put his car keys in his pockets.

'You don't have to shout.'

'I'M NOT FUCKING SHOUTING,' he shouted.

'We just got back. Aren't you tired? You've been playing all night. Besides, it's nearly two in the morning. Where are you going to go at this time of night?'

'Somebody'll be up. Yesterday was pogey day. They'll have had a chance to get to the liquor store.'

'They're no more than cronies those guys you call friends, Sandy. Drinking buddies.'

His head shot up. 'I'd give my life for any of those Jesus men,' he yelled.

'But would they do the same for you?'

'Who are you to tell me who I am?' he asked her. His voice was cold; ice on a lake in wintertime that would crack, if you stepped in the right place.

I retreated upstairs, and put my hands over my ears to stop the sounds of the crashes and her yells, but they trickled through anyway.

I found her in the kitchen, slumped in a thin pool of fluorescent white thrown by the pantry light. She hovered over a near-empty shot glass. Her hair was dishevelled and she looked cold.

'He's not a real man.' She was talking to herself again.

'Who?' I stood on the cold linoleum of the kitchen floor.

'Get something on those spakins,' she ordered. She took the slippers off her own feet and threw them to me. I put them on my feet and clambered up onto the chair opposite her.

'Who's not a real man?'

'Never you mind.' She considered something for a few seconds. 'Listen, Morag. You want to go with your grandfather, then fine, you go.'

'Go where with Grandpa?'

'You think he'll take care of you? Get you off to school on the schoolbus each morning? Do you think he'll feed you and clothe you? I'll tell you what he'll do: he'll go out drinking every night like he does now and he'll leave you alone every single night. We'll see how well you get along. And you mark my words, because I'm leaving.'

'Where are you going?'

'Never you mind. I've got plans of my own. I've got a life to live that doesn't include taking care of drunks and children. And for Jesus' sake stop crying! You're as bad as your grandfather. Here.' She shoved a box of Kleenex across the table at me. 'If you want to cry, cry into that. You get scared in the dark, remember. He'd leave you at night and come back in the morning and that would be that. He loves you only insofar as he doesn't have to deal with you. If he doesn't have to take care of you then he'll love you. If you have to take care of him then he'll hate you every inch of the way for it. Yous two are alike in one way,' she went on. She tended to lose her grammar when she drank. 'I think you both have contempt for me. Just because I'm stuck here with the two of yous on my hands. "Granma this and Christine that, gimmee this and gemme that". Well, I'm getting the hell out.'

I climbed down from the chair, started to run to my room.

'You mark my words,' she called after me.

I ran up the stairs but it was waiting for me, the creature with the body of a snake and the teeth of a barracuda. It chased me downstairs every morning and up every evening. Usually I could outrun it but tonight I tripped on the top step, and then it had me by the ankles. I screamed and fought, but it hung on with its release-hinge jaws.

My fall was broken by the door at the bottom of the staircase. My grandmother opened the door, and I tumbled out onto her feet, where I landed in a heap.

'What's the matter with you anyway?' she picked me up, sighing, tired of this nightly occurrence. 'Are you going epileptic?'

Ever since I could remember I had this picture of my life hung upside down at the back of my eye like a negative image waiting to be developed. In it I saw a horse galloping along the tracks to meet, at some unforeseen point, a freight train – the kind that Canadian National still ran at the time from Halifax through to Sydney. They were both churning toward each other, the horse rotating on the circular engine of his flanks, the train clanging, stupidly metallic. What the horse would do once it had caught the metal smell of its bulk in her nostrils I did not know. But it was a horse and a train on a flat landscape that was not home. A foreign place, like the feeling of almost-love, comfortable and uncatastrophic.

The train is just about to leave the station. The horse – the one who will run along the track to meet the train, hindquarters churning, buxom as a quarterhorse – is chewing his grass calmly with the sideways jaw-scrape assurance of predatorless creatures. In the prairie scrub-brush night they will meet, the horse witty and anarchic in its heaving flesh and the fleshless train, grinding dimly on its universe of the straight and narrow, spewing sparks like destinies. They fly off into a night which quickly absorbs their bunched-fireflies nexus of light.

Night, and the flanks of the mountains rising and falling with each breath.

When I was still a long way off and waiting to begin.

THREE

'I ALREADY told you about the melting hand.'

'Tell me again.'

He shot me a look in the mirror. 'Mind you don't fall in,' he mumbled through his mask of shaving cream.

I perched on the edge of the bathtub, just above the chainsaw, which sat in the tub. He always kept it there because he could hose the dirt off it and oil it there and it fit perfectly. I could only have baths when he was out clearing or cutting: the chainsaw had priority.

'All right,' he sighed heavily, and dutifully picked up the by-now-familiar War Narrative. 'And the sky and the ground became molten lead, and the fingers dripped off Johnny's hand, like wax when it drips down the side of a candle. My eyes were forced shut by the heat. I could feel my hair, but most of all the tiny hairs on my face, in my eyebrows, my eyelashes, burning like tinder, crackling up like little twigs ... God, I look like the wreck of the *Hesperus*,' he broke off and moaned into the mirror. He was very conscious of the fact that he had hardly any eyelashes. They had mostly been burnt off.

He stood bent into his reflection, his torso hard and white, the suspenders hanging by his thighs like a harness waiting for a horse.

These kinds of nights he would play for four or five hours straight. He would have forty dollars or so in his pocket, his small payment for playing to a field full of four or five hundred people. But then, he got his food and drink free. He was due to play at the Legion in an hour, but he was still stuck in front of the bathroom mirror.

I had an inspiration.

'You can have eyelashes,' I told him.

'How?' He squinted at me in the mirror.

I rummaged around in Grandma's drawer.

'Mascara,' I said, whipping out Grandma's 'black gold cream' wand from her bag.

He sat down on the edge of the tub. His parchment-thin eyelids fluttered as I tried to apply it to his eyelashes, which poked out of his eyelids like the dry seagrass that grew in the sand dunes down at the shore.

'There,' I said when I was finished.

'You got another one of those?' he pointed to the mascara stick.

'No. I'm too young for this. It's Grandma's.'

'Well, give us that anyway.' He plucked it from my hand.

Then he resumed his story, wagging the mascara stick in my face.

'I've seen guys tossed out of the water from the distance between here and that table over there.' He pointed out the door and across the kitchen to the far wall, a distance of some thirty yards. 'I've seen ships blow up closer than I could throw a rock, and felt the heat on my face as I ran from the railing for cover inside.

'I've seen the sea boil with the heat of burning fuel and men's limbs on fire as they tried to dive to get underneath the oil. Some made it: we'd slow down and pick them up when they came up from under the slick. Those were the good swimmers. The others just burned or drowned. "Fight on the beaches and fight in the streets." Hah,' he snorted. 'If they had ever reached the shores of England those Limeys would have been too busy figuring out which German arse to lick first.'

While he was putting on his shirt he turned around.

'You don't understand any of this, do you? Anyways,' he said, threading his cufflinks, 'I hope to see all those German bastards in very uncomfortable positions in hell when I get there.' He grinned at himself in the mirror, slapped his suspenders down on his shoulders, threw some cold water at his face, and grabbed his jacket.

'Now don't you wait up for me, you hear?' He shoved me down in a chair by the table. 'I'll go and get your grandmother.' He looked at his watch to see if she was ready to get off her shift. 'You've got to stay home with her tonight. This place I'm going is no good for kids. Understand?'

I nodded. He bounded out the door and was gone.

He always did the same thing at the end of a party or a concert when he had finished playing. He stroked the callouses on the tips and sides of his fingers carefully, taking in the full scope of their engorgement. Then he put his fiddle, accordion and guitar away, still greasy with the sweat from his fingers, wiping the body of the instruments with a cloth, packing them in their plush red and violet cases with the rapt attention someone else would give to the body of a lover.

It was the instruments to which he felt his first allegiance. But he had other lovers. They were brown-bottle-eyed women, some local, some come from languid, mist-clogged lands. They were called Schooner, Ten Penny, Moosehead, Captain Morgan's Dark. Their juices gurgled in his throat, spread upward like a stealing summer fog to where they clouded his eyes which were the same colour as icebergs at sunset, blue shadows creeping into their sharp crevices at the onset of night. He treated his lovers badly. He drank them up and spat them out.

At two in the morning Frankenstein opened the screen door. Long black lines dripped from underneath his eyes, and black was smudged into the half-moon hollows beneath his orbs.

'How do you get this stuff off?' he mumbled as we stood in front of the bathroom mirror again.

I slapped cold cream all over his eyes, as I had seen Grandma do with hers.

'Ow,' he yelled. He was jumpy with someone else around his eyes. He wasn't yet used to the rituals of makeup application.

'I've got to get some of the waterproof stuff,' he said. 'I sweat too goddamn much.'

After that he always carried mascara with him. He sometimes put it on in the car, twisting the rear-view mirror over toward him to get a good view.

They stood on the veranda, their necks craned upward like turtles.

'It's something about Mars and Venus. I heard them talking about it on CBC,' he explained. 'They're closer together than they ever have been before. I know one thing for sure: there's a Jesus lot of strange things happening up there this year.'

In July the planets of Mars and Venus were tightly drawn together in a straight alignment with Earth. They threw a light more luminous than the moon. More than once he had nearly driven off the road while looking up at them.

'Will they collide?' I asked.

'I don't know,' he shrugged. 'Maybe.'

He plucked the burning red ember of the cigarette from his mouth and threw it down on the veranda.

'Hmm, the end of the world.' He stubbed out the butt with the heel of his boot, releasing lava-red ashes that twirled like fireflies and scattered away into the night.

On the day of the eclipse we were working outside, overhauling the large vegetable patch, pulling up parsnips the size of a man's forearm.

'Do you know the hair is standing up on my arms?' She wiped the sweat off her brow and put the hoe aside. 'Here,' she thrust her arms at us. My grandfather and I peered. It was true: she was covered in goosebumps and her fine downy hair was electrified, bolt-upright.

'I'm nearly shivering myself,' he said, and lit a cigarette. 'I was thinking, what if the sun doesn't come back?'

At first we hardly noticed it, although we were tensed for some kind of sign. We had been told when it would take place, and not to look directly at the sun when it happened, or our eyes would be burnt out of our heads.

It began as a tiny sliver of darkness, more like a shadow of a giant raven stuck across the sun. Then the birds had stopped singing, as if they had all been stricken and died at once. The crickets began to chirr; the midday drowsiness changed suddenly into sleep. When the real darkness finally came, it was a curious hue, like thick tea – simultaneously dark and transparent. The tall pine trees grew fuller against the sky, their mid-afternoon shadows erased. But it was a false, mechanical night. It hovered over the island awhile, uncertain, and then was drawn back, gradually, like a velvet curtain being pulled slowly aside by a celestial hand.

We stood rapt in the fields at the end of the afternoon, a little shocked, I think, by what we had seen, by the kind of primeval dread it had nudged inside us. After it was over he eased himself down beside the vegetable patch and drew his bow-shaped legs up against his chest.

'I'm sorry she wasn't here to see it. Apparently N.S.'s the only place in the world you can see the whole sun being blotted out. They say thousands of people came up here from the States just to watch it.'

'She's on the other side of the world,' she said, raking a strand of long sweetgrass with her teeth. 'It's probably just a shadow on the sun over there.'

He flung his muscled arms out behind him and looked in the general direction of the water. The setting sun filled the lines on his face with a deep purple light.

'The way I figure it we were lucky to see the sun disappear.'

'How's that?' she raised an eyebrow. 'I thought it was spooky.'

'It's only once in a lifetime you get to see that kind of thing,' he argued. 'Like a comet streaking across the sky, the one that only comes by every seventy years or so. They used to take things like this happening in the sky as a sign of disaster.'

'Och, yes,' she flung her teeth-stripped grass away. 'But that was before people knew anything at all about the universe. Now we know it's all just natural. You're just looking for an excuse to be gloomy.'

She stood up, dusted herself off, and went into the house. He stayed by the vegetable patch, his arms around his bent legs, looking up at the sky. He stayed there until the real darkness gathered in pools around him and the mosquitoes started to eat him alive.

FOUR

'CHRISTINE.'

Great-Grandma called over her shoulder as she came in from outside, where she had been planting her purple pansies.

'Sandy says he wants to go to town.' She made for the sink to wash her hands. 'He says for you to get dressed. He'll leave in half an hour.'

'Are we going to town?'

Going to Town only happened once a month, if that, and required the forward planning of a medium-sized military expedition. We would get all our provisions, four boxes of salt in the winter in case the blizzards and roads were too bad to get through, six tubs of ice cream in summer in case we had too much work on the farm to allow us the luxury of another trip until the fall. We would go visiting, too, to see their friends. I would get candy and Grandma would buy new clothes.

I looked across the kitchen at my grandmother. Her face was lit up with the prospect of town.

'Shouldn't you be doing something?' Great-Grandma looked at me.

'Like what?'

'Like earning your dinner, maybe. You could help your grandfather out in the field.'

'Okay.'

I reached him in the field where he was scything. Rivulets of sweat ran down his bare back. He straightened up when he saw me.

'What're you doing out here?' He took his hat off his brow and tipped it at a funny angle, wiping away the sweat underneath.

'Great-Grandma told me I should come out and help you.'

'Unless you're going to cut this grass with your teeth I don't see how you can do me any good.' He looked mournfully out at the ground he had left to cover. 'Anyway,' he pointed to a pile of felled grass, 'why don't you rake that up and we'll see about getting you some proper work later on.'

Eileen was his mother, my great-grandmother. It was she who owned the house we lived in. Although she appeared as thin and brittle as a stick of glass, in reality she had the almost supernatural resilience of the tough alder bushes which continually threatened to consume our fields. Her face looked just like John Wayne's, and in its slanted angles you could see the tight and suspicious regard of someone who had spent much of her life covered in blood of one kind or another – from plucked chickens to carved-up moose, to men, presumably, as she had cooked most of her life in the winter lumber camps. If there was anything really distasteful to be done, like shooting a dog caught in a bear trap, she was the one who did it. She merely aimed the rife and shot, while the dog looked at her as any creature would look at what it recognizes as its natural assassin.

His mother had inherited the Big House – the *Tigh Mhór* in Gaelic – from one of her boyfriends, someone she had met in the lumber camps of New Brunswick or Québec. He was a fellow islander, and that must have brought them together. But come the spring he was dead, a hundred-year-old tree having fallen square on top of him. In the meantime he had left his magnificent house to her in his will. What she had done to inspire such generosity and why the man had no heirs was a mystery. But then as a people we were known for our bitter reticences and unnerving silences, so nobody asked questions.

Our home was a huge, wide-girthed house. The slats of the shutters were painted ruby red, the veranda swaddled three-quarters of the house's waist. At the back end was a rhubarb patch and a long descent down to the brook where a plum tree tipped down the bank. The corner at the back of the veranda was quiet and shaded, a kind of secret place. When the sun shone through the leaves of the giant Canadian oak, patterns of glittering mottled light spread over the floorboards like poured gold. Inside the screen windows was the dining room and its mahogany cabinets stocked with china. Every afternoon the great teak dining table became shot through with gold as the sun transformed it into a caramel colour, sweet and ripe. Around four or five o'clock in the afternoon you could almost lick the candied light off the furniture.

I had been born in this house, or so I thought. I belonged there, among the elegant spinning wheel, the dusty statues of Mounties that sat on the shelf in the kitchen, the medicinal smell of kerosene as it was poured into the heaters used to thaw out our bedrooms before we went to sleep in winter. But none of the old brittle china, none of the deep-blooded wood was ours. This all belonged to Eileen, my great-grandmother, and had belonged to her boyfriend, who was dead.

'Sandy.' Eileen came out of the house and walked toward us. 'Christine wants you to take her to town. She's all ready to go, dolled up and everything. She says for you to come in right now. You'd better come in.'

His face grew dark. He threw down his scythe. His mother trotted in front of him, I behind. We all trooped in the house together.

She stood in the middle of the kitchen. She'd put on a dress and some jewellery. She'd done her hair and makeup. Her small handbag rested hopefully on the chair.

'What the hell's this?' he exploded.

My grandmother looked confused for a moment.

'I thought you wanted to go to town . . .' she began.

'Are you daft? I'm in the middle of haying the field. What are you all dressed up for?'

My grandmother looked over to Eileen, who sat at the kitchen table with her hands folded on her lap, not looking at either of them.

'What are you trying to do to me?' he yelled. 'Do you want us to lose this hay? You know damn well I can't afford to go to town right now. Who's going to pay for the gas? It sure as hell isn't going to be you.'

'I thought . . .' she began, her voice small.

'Well you thought wrong. You're just a spoilt little girl, wanting to be taken to town in the middle of haying. What's the matter with you? Go upstairs and take those fucking fancy duds off.'

I looked at Eileen. On her face, I saw something moving, a small animal scrabbling, twisting itself in its effort to be free. Then it escaped, running across the tundra. She had a mouth that could have been carved by scythes. It blossomed there with the audacity of berries, a slaughterhouse smile.

Nobody would speak of how we had come to be here. No one, not even the real old-timers, would talk of what was known in the Highlands and Islands as *Bliadhna an Losgaidh*: the Year of the Burnings. That year, 1814, when our families had left, was the year the landlords' men set fire to the clachans, to the houses, burning the fields too, the grass of the fine greasy land, thick with peat. The crofters were turned out to make room for the *caoraich mhór*; the big sheep, who had to feed on the best of all grasses, the meadows and the *machair* along the coasts. They were traded for grasslands by those who considered them more parasitic than the Roman-nosed blackfaced sheep with yellow eyes devoid of hunger or wondering.

The Factors took advantage of the absence of the men, off fighting in the French wars, to evict the women and children.

They set fires to the roof and to the loom and they desecrated the shrine of the hearth by pouring milk onto it, so that some seventy years later, sitting in the New World, the children of those Clearances would cry at the smell of burned milk.

And when the men returned, their wives and children were simply not there anymore. Who knows which ship they had been put on? The names were incomprehensible: New Zealand, Canada, North Carolina.

When the crofters came to the shore of the New World they were simply told to get off. Often the ship captains, in a hurry to get on to Québec, would dump them short of their intended harbour, where deeds with their name and a few acres of land were printed, patiently waiting. They were left in the forest, short of their land. They carried their belongings, the few potatoes they had saved for planting, a trunk or two, and plunked them on the shore. As night fell they made for the woods, where they had to cut down the trees to make a lean-to; eventually a shack.

The mystery is, how did they manage this without an axe? They, forebears of men who would one day be lumberjacks, would not have brought one with them, for the simple reason that they had no such tool. There were no trees left in the Highlands.

FIVE

H E plunked a cardboard box down on the floor, thrust his cigarette in his mouth and went to take off his lumberjack shirt. A thin whimper came from inside the box.

'Is it hurt?'

He was always bringing home injured animals and fixing them up or taking them to the vet in Sydney Mines. We once had a fox for three weeks. He'd found it with a broken front leg, made a splint himself and fed the animal until the bone healed.

'No,' he said, wrestling with his shirt. 'It's a dog.'

We had run out of Rexes, all big German Shepherds. Rex 1 was hit by a lumber truck. Rex 2 got caught in a bear trap and had to be shot. I forget what happened to Rex 3; maybe a mountain lion got him. After he was killed we got a bitch, the one in the box, and he couldn't reasonably call her Rex.

He stood scratching his head, looking down at her in the cardboard box, where she lay all curled up just like the fox he had brought home.

'Well, what are you looking at?' he challenged. 'I'm trying to figure out what we're going to name the Jesus thing. You're smart,' he told me. 'You think of something.'

At the precise moment he uttered the word 'smart' the dog opened one chocolate eye, very lazy, and looked up at him. She gave him such a look of recognition it was obvious she knew everything before we did.

That day he named her *Marag*, the Gaelic word for black

pudding, a sausage-like substance made from cow's blood. I can understand how he arrived at this word; she was black as coal. But he forgot how close the word was to my name; only one vowel separated us. So that when they called to me, she would turn around too. When they shouted at the dog, I flinched.

As it turned out, she was very smart. When she got older the dog would sit on the kitchen floor, head cocked in one direction, watching them go back and forth at each other as if she were watching a tennis match. Then, when he broke loose, she went in there to my grandmother's defence. The dog and the underdog, fighting together.

The dog kept an eye on him. All animals can feel earthquakes coming, often as much as half an hour in advance. She was a seismograph; she would begin to flinch and twitch in advance, her little needle of a nose registering the coming bucking peaks and valleys of feeling. She had her nose to the ground, to the subterranean magma rivers in the bowels of their love.

She stood beside the board, what looked like a thin piece of plywood, only it was dark green.

'I'm going to teach you to read, so you won't be the odd one out when you go to school.'

In her hand was a box of coloured chalk. She began to write letters, and to recite them to me. She gave me a notebook to copy them down in. Then she did simple sums. The dog and I sat on the border of the kitchen and dining room, our heads cocked in opposite directions.

'You should be able to read before you go to school,' she said. 'You're a year behind already. Everybody else will be older than you and I don't want you to feel like you're stupid. And just because we don't have any money doesn't mean you have to go ignorant.'

She went over to the little table. 'Why don't we use the *Reader's Digests*?' she suggested. 'Or we could try the Bible.' She fingered a Gideon's edition that some man in a matching grey suit and car had sold us once. 'But I think the print's too small,' she frowned.

The *Reader's Digests* won out as textbooks. Most of the True Adventure stories were dumb, depicting endless miraculous rescues from disasters. I thought people who deliberately gave themselves thrills doing things like whitewater rafting got what they deserved. But I liked the ones in which people got eaten by polar bears.

My grandfather brought in grapes from the fields so that I could make my own wine. My grandmother ground me flour and yeast, so that I could rise. They were stocking my store. The shelves were filled to bursting. Later I would be able to take from the sagging shelves and give to others.

When he and I came back that day, years later, I went there, to the storage shed. Just as I got close a long black snake shot out. It was the colour of asphalt with a yellow stripe down its back. It looked like the Trans-Canada Highway, and it was huge.

I could see the things that were rightfully mine through the window. They had already grown dusty, but all the same I wanted to take them with me.

The snake had curled itself around the tree.

'You get away,' I told the snake.

It watched me. Its flicking tongue said: *I've been waiting for you.*

I dodged the snake and tried the door.

It was locked.

'Morag.'

It was my grandmother calling from behind the screened window to where I stood at the shed.

The dog and I turned around in tandem.

'Come and eat,' she called. 'Come on and eat, both of yous.'

The dog and I bounded across the field together.

I thought they were like time itself as measured by the Long

Count practised by the ancient Maya. I thought they were without beginning or end, a continual cyclic reality. Much later I was shocked to learn there was a time, submerged somewhere in that formlessness before the year I began, when they did not even know of the other's existence.

When he met her, he knew, because everything was there, all the details. The trembling knees of the first encounter, the terror of the act and the mesmerizingly sinister properties of the Other.

What would you do, he thought, thinking of her figure, *with a body that different? What would it mean to have that body, to inhabit it forever?*

When he first saw her, she looked just like him. She was wearing a lumberjack shirt and smoking a pipe. He thought: *Who's that crazy young girl? Does she want to be a boy, or what?*

The next time he saw her was at Christmas, and she wore a green dress and coloured beads for a necklace and tied her curly anarchic hair up with a dark green velvet ribbon. And someone told him, 'Sandy, that's the girl who goes around with her father in the woods in winter. He lets her wear a lumberjack shirt and even lets her smoke.'

He thought of his own mother, standing in her corduroy trousers, woollen socks and tough leather boots in a New Brunswick logging camp, leaning her thin breast-less frame against one of the condemned trees, its trunk stripped and sapless, closing her eyelids and letting snowflakes drop onto them and feeling the rate at which they succumbed to her body's heat.

It was when he met her that Christmas at the party and asked her to dance that he saw the grey slate of her eyes. He looked deep into them, and in seeing their unusual colour, a combination of wet graphite and charcoal, he felt he might have fallen down onto rough stone and skinned his knees. They looked like pools of water frozen into thin ice, the kind men broke and fell through on the lake during the first and last days of winter.

He thought: flint.

He thought: you could sharpen a knife on those eyes.

AUTUMN

SIX

'OFF to the Asylum with yez,' he chuckled. He bent down to button up my new cardigan.

'That's not funny, Sandy,' she glared at him. 'She doesn't know what calling it an Asylum means. She's scared enough. You'll only confuse her.'

'She's not half as confused as she'll be in school. They aren't fit for pigs – it's the same thing: fat little things grunting and shoving each other around to get at the trough.'

'No wonder you never went further than the eleventh grade.'

'You didn't neither,' he reminded her.

School was a square, ranch-style building two or three miles down the road from the *Tigh Mhór*. Across the green fibreglass siding stretched the letters LIT BO R CON OLODAT D. The name hadn't been fixed in ten years. Everyone knew what it was anyway. It was The Asylum.

Almost immediately, the Mad found me.

'You're a bastard,' the kid with the screwed-up face and thin brown hair that wouldn't comb right sneered. 'Where's your father?'

'My grandfather's up at the *Tigh Mhór*.'

'Not your grandfather,' the kid sneered. 'Your *father*. Your grandfather's too old.'

The fizz of doubt in my stomach.

'Teacher, I don't feel well.'

'Sit down, then,' said Mrs Chisholm. 'We're going to colour in mice.'

39

I had never coloured in anything before. It seemed a strange thing to do. The mouse in question looked nothing like the mice I had seen, bloodied and crushed between the cat's paws, or fleeing snakes mad in pursuit.

'I want you to use grey for the fur and pink for the ears.'

When we had done we each had to go to the front of the room to show our mice.

'Turn and face the Class, Morag,' the teacher said, as I handed in mine. I turned, my bright pink trousers and my thin white bargain-store cardigan making me a lighthouse in front of the bobbing sea of faces.

'Now look, Class, because Morag hasn't done hers properly. She's coloured in circles instead of up and down lines and the colour has gone outside of the boundaries. You'll do better next time, won't you, Morag?'

I looked at her from my position, high up above the waves. My face was blank as the revolving light of many mirrors, each differently angled.

'Won't you, Morag?' Mrs Chisholm stood up now, her hands on her hips.

'Are you going to hit me?' I asked, still in my beacon posture.

Mrs Chisholm flushed deep red.

'No, I'm not going to hit you,' she kept her voice low. 'Now who gave you the idea that anyone would do that?'

I didn't move, or say anything.

'You may sit down, Morag.'

'I think I should have a talk with your grandparents.'

Mrs Chisholm had kept me after class.

'Do your grandparents ever hit you?' She fidgeted with her pen, turning it around and around.

'No.'

I had never had anyone ask me about my grandparents before. Her question seemed spiked with possible dangers.

'Well, where did you get the idea that someone would hurt you?' she asked gently.

'You were mad at me.'

'You're not supposed to take these things personally. It was just a colouring exercise. All you have to do is learn to keep the colour inside the boundaries. Is that so hard?' She sat back.

So she drove me home in her clapped-out yellow Volkswagen beetle, home to Grandma and the snakes and the dog; to where uncertainty was predictable in that it was what happened when he came home at night.

Snapshot: a girl stands outside, next to the highway. Her black hair has been cut short recently, her bangs float in the wind. She wears a thin white cardigan bought at a discount store in Sydney Mines and a pair of pink and white trousers. Her shoes are brown and white leather saddle shoes, bought especially for school. She carries a leather satchel which smells the deep, mellow animal scent of new leather. It has been specially made for her by a friend of Chief Dan's on the reservation.

Her dog waits by her side, patiently, for something to happen. The dog knows this day is different, and things will not be the same again. Her grandfather fetches his mother's old Hasselblad camera, one of those that you have to look down into, a mirror showing you the picture ahead. The girl poses awkwardly with her satchel, waiting for the camera to click, waiting for her grandfather to straighten up and tell her that she can move now. As her grandfather presses the shutter the wind comes like an animal charging out of the woods and sweeps its paw against her face. Her short hair is lifted, suspended, as are the edges of her white knit cardigan, the one that has been bought at the discount store in Sydney Mines where the window displays are never changed and everything has faded to a generic yellowish-orange.

Finally, the school bus comes. Its yellow form devours the turn in the road above the *Tigh Mhór*. It thunders to a stop and, with a final grinding of gears, flips open its doors. She walks in, and is immediately consumed by chaos. She finds an empty seat and crams herself in against the window. Outside, in front of the house, stand her grandmother, her grandfather, and her dog. The dog is barking wildly. Her grandmother looks pleased, as if she has just accomplished something. Her grandfather stubs out his cigarette with his foot, grins and waves to her. His heavy woollen shirt is open to reveal his white undershirt. For the first time in her life, in the midst of all these children who have their eyes fixed upon the spectacle outside, which constitutes her one and only world, she senses, rather than knows, that she ought to feel embarrassment.

He staggered in the door. Dirt – soot or oil – was streaked across his face, and one of the elbows of his shirt was torn out, so that his white elbow poked through like a broken bone.

'What happened to you?'

'Oh, nothing. Bit of an accident,' he said, in a by-the-by tone. He sat down at the table and began to roll a cigarette.

'Where's the car?' I asked, peering out the door.

'On the South Side.' He licked the side of his roll-up.

'How did you get here?'

'What is this, twenty questions?'

He cupped his hand over the end of the roll-up to light it. There was no wind in the kitchen: this was a gesture of habit, acquired from too many years lighting too many cigarettes out in the open. He took his first drag.

'Well, I'll tell you then, since you're so eager to know: I walked.'

'From where?'

'The South Side. All twelve miles. And that was after me crawling out of the side window of the car, upside down in the ditch. And,' he added smoothly, wagging his cigarette at me, 'I was stone cold sober.'

This was a new twist. I'd been in the ditch with him plenty of times already. I could have been forgiven for thinking that was the whole purpose of having a car: to drive it off the road. Usually, though, there was a half-drunk forty-ouncer bottle of rum rolling around in the trough, where it had slipped out of the lopsided car as we made our escape. Holding his bloody nose he would make straight for the brackish water where the rum bottle lay, half-submerged in the stagnant ooze. 'Can't let this go to waste,' he would say, plucking it out.

'So what happened?'

He puffed on his roll-up twice before answering, pausing for dramatic effect.

'A moose ran out in front.'

'Is the moose all right?'

'He's fine. Bit bruised, I imagine, but fine. You should see the car though . . . ooh.' He sucked his breath in through his teeth and shook his head. 'Totalled. Absolutely totalled. My God, them are big animals. I went right over, arse to elbow.' He tumbled his hands over one another to demonstrate the somersault motion. 'But there's not even a scratch on me, look.' He stubbed out his cigarette in the ashtray and stood up, arms and legs spread as if he was about to be frisked.

I looked him over. It was true. Not a scratch.

'Yeah, well, you know me, tough as nails.' He sat down heavily. 'That walk's just played me out,' he said, and fell right asleep.

He was still there when she came home from her evening shift at the motel restaurant.

'What happened to him?' She gestured to the slumped figure in the chair as I unzipped the back of her waitress uniform.

When she had heard the story she pursed her lips and frowned.

'I think we should have him checked out to see that it's really flesh he's got on those bones.'

She sat down on the brown vinyl chair across from him, rubbed her knees and sighed, a great disappointed sound dispersing itself through the silent kitchen, disproportionately loud and forlorn, sounding, in its intensity, not unlike the wounded cry of a moose.

SEVEN

CRACK!
  'Goddamn it – missed her,' he swore.
  'Easy, Sandy,' Dan soothed. 'Let me have a go.'
Crack!

I cringed, along with the trees, who shouted back their indignation with a sharp echo.

'Dammit.'

The doe galloped, head held high, straight through the forest. I saw her white rear fly gracefully over a fallen log, and then she was gone.

'Let's have some more bullets then, Morag,' Grandpa yelled and I came trotting out of the woods, the cartridges heavy in my palm.

'Well-trained, she is,' Dan sighed. 'Jesus more use than my boy, that's for sure.' He paused to light a cigarette, his tall broad frame bent in the single purpose of getting a flame. He turned his back toward the wind and lit his cigarette. The blue smoke mingled with his condensed breath.

'Got into drinking already,' Dan continued, 'and him only thirteen.'

'They just don't know what to do with themselves,' he told Dan, slinging his gun over his right shoulder and kicking at the frosted ground with his steel-toed boots. 'Not enough to worry about so they have to cause trouble.'

Dan grunted. 'Don't know where Paul's going to go to.' He

looked into the sky, squinting against the coming twilight. His grey hair, nearly shoulder length but tied back, bobbed up and down with his movements. 'Too much working against him.'

My grandfather nodded. 'Did you tell him smoking and drinking will stunt his growth?'

'If I told him he'd be a goddamn midget whose only paid employment would be begging a buck for a bottle of aftershave on some Toronto street corner he still wouldn't pay any attention.'

Dan's gaze settled delicately, like a feathery grouse dropping down in the grass to nest, somewhere in the far distance.

'She's over there,' Dan said quietly, cradling the gun more snugly in the crook of his arm.

'You's got a better instinct in the woods than me,' said my grandfather, smiling at Dan. 'It's because you's Indian.'

Dan winced. 'Don't give me that Indian bullshit, Sandy,' he grumbled. 'It's 'cause I've been around longer, that's all. I'm gettin' old, b'y.'

Big Dan was just what his name implied. Broad-shouldered, over six feet tall, he had wide-sprung cheekbones on top of which he wore square-ish eyeglasses. He was the chief of the local band of Micmac, and lived on the reservation, which was strung out on both sides of the Trans-Canada Highway in a wide bay about an hour from the island. He and my grandfather had both invested in the reservation oyster farm since they had worked together at the naval base after the war.

I jogged behind them to keep up, hoping all the time that the deer had run far away.

'Shh,' they both turned toward me in unison. 'Don't make a sound now,' Grandpa hissed. 'We're coming into the clearing.'

The doe was there, nervously grazing off the low branches of trees that still had foliage on them. I began to sweat in my down-filled coat. I could smell it, her death: her body still warm and her noise moist, prone on the forest floor. I hung back in the trees, underneath the wide grey-helmeted sky, threatening to fall in an hour, when the autumn dusk would come. Dan paused while my grandfather went on a few steps. We watched his green and check hunting jacket disappear into the thicket, from where he would get a fix on the doe. Beside me, Dan shivered.

'I don't care for hunting at dusk. Must have something to do with stories Dad used to tell me. Dusk's the time of the Trickster,' he explained, lighting another cigarette. 'It's the hour of change, just before night especially. The Trickster comes then. He knows we're confused.'

'Confused about what?'

Dan shot two thin streams of blue smoke from his nostrils and shrugged. 'About everything.'

'The night's when God clamps a big lobster pot lid down on the sky and that's why there's no light.'

Dan looked down at me. 'Who told you that bullshit?'

'My grandfather.'

'Hey,' he called to us, waving his orange hunting cap to get our attention. 'Let's go, you two. We're not here to chew the goddamn fat.'

In school we were taught about the finesse of the Micmac, their skill in fishing and hunting, as well as the total annihilation the Newfoundland Beothuks suffered at the hands of our ancestors, the white men. We were taught something of the superiority and the economy of the Algonquin way of life; we learned the strange bubbling-syllable names that marked the way through the dense woods and geography of our existence – *Kejimkujik, Nyanza, Shubenacadie, Whycocomagh*. We learned these alongside the names of places in our own language – Margaree, Liverpool, Inverness, Cheticamp, Halifax, Belle Côte: the Micmac, the Scots, the French and the English.

But when we went to the reserve to visit Dan we entered by driving a roadside gauntlet of dusty shops full of baskets and beads sold to the tourists who stop on the highway. The houses on the reservation were crumbling, ramshackle, low-slung wooden prefabs. Some of them had only tar paper roofs. Children sat listless on their doorsteps only to run across the highway suddenly, dodging cars in a game of chicken. Dogs ambled along the roadside with that skipping hyena gait all hungry animals have. Parts of cars and rusted motorcycles embedded themselves in driveways.

How had this happened? Where were the fierce, sinuously muscled warriors of our history books? Where was the pemmican and the teepees? Now the only birch-bark tent was erected beside Googoo's souvenir shop. (*Get your picture taken with the Chief! in the teepee beside the Handee basket and bead shoppe!*) And some American would wander into the teepee where Charles MacRae or another assimilated-named Micmac like Dan would be sitting with a dime-store headdress on in the gloom.

Flash!

Real Indian Chief!

What had happened? No matter how many history books we read in school it seemed there was only one story to our country, but its name was forever obscured in the snowdrifts that smothered the years between our arrival and their demise.

When it is that still, the air swallows a bullet's crack without a trace, as if the sound has been smothered in the felt of isolation. And you hear it going, that leaping projectile of thrust, and you know it takes years for a bullet, once launched, to sink into the flesh of its destination. Dynasties rise and fall, centuries decay into backwardness, iron rusts and becomes element again with the soil. The bullet rifles slowly, turning once for every year it has taken to build the species – whether it be bird, reptile, mammal.

That evening I saw a deer killed. That evening before my grandfather aimed and fired – something I always liked to watch and even admired, the precision, the exactitude, the velocity – I felt something turn over inside me. A liquid, like that in the brown eye of the deer, moved. My feet grew hoofs and my ankles fetlocks, my nose became moist and trembling. I could smell it: the phosphorus ripping into flesh, my organs pummelled and burnt by a projectile that came from no part of my ante-diluvian memory, nearly as old as the oldest creatures on the earth. The liquid in my eye turned to stone, my feathered fetlocks wilted. I was cold, as if my blood had stopped flowing. I heard a collective wail build in my ears, and then a whoosh like the Atlantic belting our shore in a January storm.

I was expected to learn to shoot and to hunt. How could I ever kill, if I was the quarry? I heard the shot again, making its return journey from thrust back into the relevance of death. And then the deer crumpled as if she had never existed, and her white tail went down.

They wrestled the deer onto the long hood of the Ford Falcon and tied it there.

'Fuckin' pickup's on the blink,' Grandpa swore, sweating with ropes and antlers and the ripped fur of the carcass.

'Would've been a lot easier to put her in the back of the truck,' Dan agreed, fighting with the doe's hind leg, which kept slipping over the side and into the wheel base.

He brushed his gloved hands clean after securing the last rope around the front fender. 'Well, there's our meat for a couple of months. Here,' he called to me. His voice was as sharp as gunshot. 'Put that in the trunk.' He tossed the smaller rifle, the .22.

I caught the rifle but it knocked me down. He looked over to where I lay in a dusty heap on the gravel, looking surprised but simultaneously uninterested, as if he had momentarily for-gotten me. I lay flat out on my back for a few moments, my eyes full of sky.

Dan ran over and relieved me of the gun.

'What's the matter with you?' he yelled over his shoulder at my grandfather. 'Chucking the rifle at her? It could have gone off. You're treating her like she's a full-grown man. She's only a small thing yet.' Dan plucked the rifle from across my chest, hauled me up by the arm and we drove home, my grandfather navigating the road through the antlers of the deer, who sailed in front of us on our hood like an elaborate figurehead on a Viking longboat.

We brought the deer home for her to skin and prepare. She met us as we pulled into the driveway. She looked at it with distaste, its purple-black tongue lolling over the side of the hood to where it hung just above the signal light.

'This'll take me all night,' she lamented. 'I have to go down to the motel tonight.'

'Well, it's your friggin' job.'

Dan gave her an apologetic smile. 'I'll give you a hand, Christine,' he offered.

'Don't you dare,' Grandpa commanded. 'We've done our bit. This is women's work and we're going to sit down and have a beer.'

'Jesus, Sandy.' Dan looked down at him as if he were a child. 'What century are you living in? Nothing's just women's work anymore. The three of us will get this done quicker and then we can all have a beer.'

Dan and Grandma dragged the carcass off to the very edge of the veranda. My grandmother knelt, her still-dark hair falling over her face, with the carving knife above the doe while Dan got down on the ground and knelt holding the deer at his chest. She cut and he pulled the skin away. I stood behind the screen door, watching the blood flow down the veranda toward me.

'Do you want the deerskin for your bed, Morag?' Grandpa asked from behind me. He put his hands on my shoulders. They smelled of gunshot.

I shook my head and ran to my room.

The three rabbit skins on my bed quivered, and I was underneath the covers. It was seven in the evening, and I fell asleep.

'Come on, let's go to the Legion. There's nothing doing around here,' my grandfather said.

Dan didn't move, or say anything.

'I'm bored, Dan,' he almost pleaded. 'Come on.'

Dan pushed his rum glass around on the table. 'I haven't got no place in that Legion of yours, Sandy,' he said, quietly, keeping his eyes fixed on the chocolate-coloured liquid.

'What do you mean?'

'Sandy, how can you be so goddamn naive? Didn't you ever notice I never go there?' Dan folded his arms and sat back in the chair in defensive posture. 'In the first place, I may have worked at the base but I never fought in any white man's war. What would I go and spill my guts out on some foreign mud swamp for the white man for? I'd have to be crazy.'

'I only meant we might go out for a drink.'

'Well, I'm not welcome in that goddamn Legion of yours, if you've got to know. I went in there one night when we were out on the town, me and some of my white buddies from Washabuck. Well, we went in the door, and it was so smoky I couldn't see a goddamn thing. But those guys sure as hell saw. They dropped their jaws as soon as they saw me in the doorway. Place went dead as a doornail. I felt like I was in a scene from *Once Upon a Time in the West*.'

'And then?' Grandpa asked.

'My buddies asked for a drink. And you know what the bartender said?' Dan looked at us, wide-eyed.

Grandpa and I shook our heads.

'He said to my buddies: "I'll get you guys your drinks, but tell the Indian that we're not serving him in here." And my buddies said, "You look here, he's no drunk, he's the Chief," and the bartender said, "I don't care if he's Geronimo at Little Big Horn, b'y. I'm not servin' no Indian any drink," and my buddies and me, we left, just like that.'

Dan's hands took flight in the air, and he waved them on either side of his head in a strange undulating gesture. 'Wouldn't serve me a drink because he thinks just because I'm an Indian I'm a . . .'

'But, Dan,' Grandpa interrupted, 'there's plenty that are, you have to admit it.'

Dan shoved his glasses further up his nose. The lenses were getting steamed up. 'I'll tell you what I've got to Jesus admit,' he said, his voice rising. 'I'll admit that those other assholes in the Legion are more drunks than I am, and that you know nothing about what makes an Indian drink. So you can get off your high horse. I know more about it than you'll ever know.'

I had never seen them argue before. Grandpa stared at the table.

'Wrote to the MP about the bartender and do you think that politician did anything about it? Charter of so-called Human Rights in this country.' Dan got up, rose to his full height, a twirling helix of contained energy, and for a minute did not seem to know what to do. He looked about the room, his brown eyes swivelling from corner to corner. He stamped his foot hard on the kitchen floor, let out a low moan, and sat back down.

My grandfather looked in my direction.

'Shouldn't you be in bed?'

I shook my head. I knew he liked me to be there, despite his desultory reprimand. I stayed with them at the table, wrapped in an old blanket, peering at them over the lips of beer bottles on the table.

Finally they decided to start a crib game.

'Moose hunting used to take two guys,' Dan was explaining as he shuffled the cards. 'They'd go out about this time of year, hang around a lake. One of the guys would fake a female moose call in an old birchbark horn. Then, when they were sure the bull was interested the other guy would get out a little dipper and start pouring water into the lake. Do you know what that was for? That,' Dan snorted and laughed, 'was to simulate the sound of a female urinating. Apparently that was what really got the bulls going. Then when he came charging from the woods they'd drive him into the shallow water and spear him there. Pretty smart, eh?'

'The ingenuity,' my grandfather shook his head in admiration.

'You know, we even had slaves.' Dan dealt us the cards. 'Not too many people know that today. I guess it's considered something to be ashamed of these days. When they took war prisoners they mostly killed them, the men anyways. Sometimes they gave men prisoners to the women to torture. I'd hate to think what they did to the poor buggers,' he shivered.

'What's torture?' I asked, scanning my cards.

'It's when you're not nice to someone,' my grandfather said.

'It's not,' Dan chided him. 'Tell her the truth.'

'It's when you hurt someone deliberately, okay?' he gave in.

'But the women and children were usually adopted by the people,' Dan went on. 'They weren't called slaves. That's what they were though, and if they ever tried to escape they were killed. Anyway,' he said, sitting back in his chair and folding his arms across his chest, 'it was a long time ago that they were in a position to feed slaves. We were finished by my grandfather's time. They got them with drink, the buggers. Do you know they used to do the same thing the English did out on the plains?'

Grandpa stubbed out his cigarette. 'What was that?'

'They used to leave cases of liquor right on the shore, just as the English did out west where they plunked them right down on the Prairie.'

'Tsk, tsk,' my grandfather clicked his tongue.

'They did just that here on the shore. And then they'd wait for the Micmac to find them. When they were good and drunk the English would do what they liked with them. But they had to be careful, because the men were terrifying when they were drunk. I remember my grandmother telling me that the Micmac women would hold their drinking parties out in the woods, a good ways away from the men, because they were so scared of their craziness when they were at the drink. Shit,' Dan exclaimed, throwing away his extra cards. 'What a piss-poor hand.'

'But then the women would get at the grog too,' he continued. 'And you know what? The fishermen around these parts, they knew about these women's parties and passed the word. Boatfuls of men would arrive and take advantage of them.'

My grandfather looked down into his glass. Those were his ancestors, very likely; the fishermen who raided the women's drinking parties; the men with thick fish-slab fingers, the men with the cracked-blue eyes of the centuries-dead genetic swirl of Norsemen and Macedonians.

'But, my God,' Dan exclaimed, sucking in his breath backwards as my grandmother sometimes did. 'They took to the grog. My own grandfather said you'd never believe the way the men carried on when they were at the bottle. And he was a proud man. He didn't like talking about the drink – as far as he was concerned that was the end of the peoples. He said at first you never heard of those drunken fights that ended up with someone being killed – those came later, when everybody was dying of liver poisoning or the flu. Before things got ugly they sang and danced and laughed like children, and them grown men, all of them. One drop of the stuff and they were in fits of giggles. They had no resistance to it, you see,' Dan explained. 'Their bodies had no ancestral memory of the alcohol.'

A diaphanous look spread itself across his eyes.

'Isn't it sad,' Dan's voice negotiated the forest of their accumulated beer bottles, 'how a people can be enslaved by euphoria?'

EIGHT

'Iᴛ's herself,' someone shouted from the smoke-clouded room. My grandmother came over to me. 'What are you doing up?'

I rubbed my eyes. 'You woke me up.'

'Come and sit on my lap.' She guided me through the smoke.

'You always have fun when I'm asleep,' I complained.

'Shush and listen to the music,' she said, lifting me onto her knee.

A call came from the crowd. 'Give us that tune Sandy – "Bog an Lochan".'

Obliging, he hauled off the heavy accordion, with its red-marbled enamelled sides, its beautifully white gleaming teeth, and reached for his fiddle. Behind him lay a six-stringed acoustic guitar which he had bought in a music shop in Sydney. Next to that his electric guitar, its spats-like design of curvy panels white on black.

When he came to the end of his tune he turned his watery eyes meanderingly in my direction.

'Why don't you give us a bit of the Sword Dance, Morag?' my grandfather asked.

'Does she know how already?' some indulgent adult marvelled.

'She's after learning at the Gaelic College,' my grandmother shoved me off her knee. 'She goes once a week.'

I looked uncertainly at my grandfather from where I stood in the middle of the room.

'What in the name of Jesus is the matter?' He was ready to go. He hated being held up when he was playing.

'We haven't got any swords.'

'Well, just imagine them.'

'I can't. It doesn't work.'

He shot up from the sofa. 'For the love of Jesus,' he swore and disappeared upstairs. He returned within seconds, carrying the .22 and the .303 rifles.

'Are you going to shoot me?'

'No, I'm going to put these on the floor and you can use them as swords,' he said, laying the rifles across one another at right angles. He picked up his fiddle.

At the Gaelic College we practised with lines of masking tape. I have never danced with swords before, let alone rifles. I jumped even higher than usual because I knew they were loaded.

'Good b'y, Morag.' I got a round of applause at the end.

At the end of the evening he would sing a maudlin song, usually a New World ballad like the 'Flying Cloud', a sad twenty-six-verse-long story of a young Maritimer who gets caught up with the pirates of the Spanish Main. He ends up being hanged at Valparaíso or Havana; I forget which. The worst thing was when Grandpa himself cried while singing. Then his voice cracked like old plaster and the song was ruined.

'You should have been Frank Sinatra,' someone joked.

'Yeah, well,' he dismissed the compliment. 'I always said that Frank Sinatra is to singing what diarrhoea is to shit.'

The music had stopped. Everyone had left. There was only a mad animal rumbling around downstairs.

'I'm afeared for you, Sandy.'

'I don't need your fear.'

Bitch, Cunt, Whore. It was the refrain of the Drunk Mass, involving the Litany of Regret and the Gospel of Gloom. They knew all the lines, all the responses. Downstairs in the kitchen she stood facing him like the wall of Jerusalem, simply shining with anger. She was more afraid for his soul than him.

I was going to defend her; myself I wasn't worried about.

'I'm going to kill him,' I thought.

But morning came, and he was always alive. And I was always relieved to find him that way.

'I don't know how I came by it,' he is saying. His palms are laid flat on his knees, his fingers lightly hugging their curve.

'I was born with it, I guess. I was born with the music and that's my delight.'

He grips his cigarettes unusually; he always has. He holds them screwed into his third and fourth fingers, torqued tighter than torsion bars. The smoke wafts upward and clouds his eyes. He never seems to notice the smoke.

'You see . . .' he looks at me '. . . some people are born with the gift for words, for language. And that's wonderful too, that's their delight. Others are good with animals. I've seen men that can take any animal in their arms and calm it right down. Some women were made to heal people, you know, be nurses and the like. Faith Healers. It's all a delight to them who can do it.'

He shoves the cigarette in his mouth and screws up his face. With his two hands proffered he leans over and picks up one of his instruments. The guitar, the fiddle, the accordion. He picks it up in his two hands as if the instrument had grown there; the shape of his fingers is in the wood memory of the fiddle.

This is merely a man explaining – or trying to explain – the inexplicable. So he invents this story of the delights handed to him and to others in the womb; theirs, outside their choosing.

It is an old myth, and I believe it.

As the nights became colder on the long slide down into winter we sat nearer and nearer the coal stove in the kitchen until the table was a distant country on the other side of the room. We drank our tea near the stove; we did the washing near the stove; we would have slept near the stove had there been room. And it was there we sat when all the lights had been turned out, except for one.

The light came from the small projector. It wheezed away on a chair in the middle of the kitchen. It threw a mottled white beacon, and dust danced through its shafts. Then she put a slide in one of the two little windows, and the light burst into colour. Vivid blue, like the northern summer sky for the water. Dripping green, as when the June rains came and the plum tree flowered for the trees. Dried-blood-brown wood and earth; colours not at all like our red clay soil.

And a woman on the jetty, in front of the river. A long piece of cloth wrapped around her, from her shoulders to her knees. It fell in as many colours as the river and the sky and the blade-leafed trees in the picture. This was taken in front of a river whose name began with Z on a continent whose name sounded warm and thick, like a carpet in winter.

Outside the snowdrifts crept up to the big white house, and the moon fell through the frozen limbs of the trees. Icebergs broke loose from their moorings and drifted by in the night sea.

My grandmother and I sat alone in the kitchen. My grandfather had gone out. Usually he never missed a slide show, but tonight he had to play. We watched the woman on the white wall. Strange animals came to stand by her side: monkeys, giraffes, and the lions she said lived practically in her back yard.

'Those animals are as old as the earth,' my grandmother told me. 'Did you know all the animals in North America crossed over from Asia?' she asked me.

'No.'

'Well, they did. And before that they walked all the way from Africa.'

Then the woman and the paintbox colours disappeared from the wall, and the snowdrifts crept away, and the winter wind moved on toward Greenland, leaving only a white square of light on the wall and the projector humming.

'Time for bed,' she announced. 'Maybe she'll send us more slides next month.'

We climbed the staircase, her presence protecting me from the nocturnal attentions of the snake/barracuda creature. At the top step Bridget's graduation photograph came into view. Her face had a creamy texture, and her light blue eyes were wrinkle-less, forever twenty-one years old. Her face bore the serious expression expected of graduates, but her mouth smiling wryly, very little. Sometimes I felt I was the only one who could see it.

'Look, Grandma, Bridget's smiling.'

'No she's not,' she said, nudging me into my bedroom. 'It's just your imagination. She's looking off into the distance.'

I struggled with my nightdress. 'What's she looking at?'

'I don't know.' She crammed the blankets around my neck, strangling me. 'Her future, I guess. Now go to sleep before your grandfather comes home.'

NINE

'I'M off for a shoot. Where's the fuckin' dog?' Eileen, her wiry grey hair spiralling out in all directions from under her huntsman's cap, stood in the porch with a 410 shotgun and a .22 rifle thrown casually over her shoulder.

'Take me, Great-Grandma, take me,' I pleaded.

'All right, you're as good as any of those idiot dogs.' Eileen spat her wad of tobacco out expertly, making a clean arc which just managed to avoid her right foot. 'They'll only maul the bird.'

I put on my boots and we went out into the hay field, now dull brown in the late autumn. We tramped through moss and bracken until we came to the edge of a field.

'Now look.' She thrust the 410 into my hands. I nearly fell down. It felt like carrying a cold metal elephant. I had never held one on my own before.

'You hold it like this . . .' And she demonstrated with the .22, stretching her arm out and her finger on an invisible trigger.

'I know how you hold it,' I complained. I went hunting with my grandfather every week and I had eyes in my head.

'You look straight down the line,' she instructed. 'And you aim an inch in front of what you're shooting at, and you follow it, because by the time the shot gets there you'll have lost an inch. Two inches if it's running.'

I nodded, the gun big and clumsy in my hands. I could barely lift it to shoulder height.

'And this is only for shotguns: rifles are different.' She shoved me up against the nearest tree so that my shoulder dug into the bark.

'When you're still young you back yourself up against a tree so you can take the kickback, hear? That way it won't knock you down. You'll just have to pick the bark out of your back.'

She plucked the gun out of my wobbling hands and lifted it expertly onto her own shoulder.

'You're ready to learn to shoot now.' She squinted down the line. 'The earlier the better as far as I'm concerned. Gives you a chance to develop your eye.' Eileen was a crack shot. My grandfather liked to tell his amazed buddies that his own mother could out-aim him any day.

'Don't you have to be old before you can have a gun?' I thought you had to be at least sixteen, and needed a licence like Grandpa had.

'Not out in the middle of fucking nowhere you don't,' she laughed, a strange light crackling through her thin blue eyes. 'Those lawmakers don't know their arse from their elbow. What's the use of waiting until you're sixteen to learn to shoot? You're practically dead by then. Your grandfather's going to start teaching you to shoot this winter. You can't expect him to put food on the table forever, you know.'

The wind spiralled around the trees and hit our faces.

'Now run ahead, just in a straight line, toward that tree.' She pointed to the far side of the clearing.

'Are you going to shoot me?'

'No, I'm going to shoot the bird.' She twirled the .22 rifle over her shoulder and set it snug into firing position. 'Now get going.'

So I ran, and sure enough, a partridge took flight at my coming footsteps. I watched its takeoff until it was well above my head, and then lowered my eyes.

Crack!

A soft, floury thud, not too far away. I stood still while my great-grandmother went to get the bird. She came back toward me, holding it upside down by the feet. Blood spattered onto her black woodman's boots. She saw my face.

'You needn't look melancholy,' she said. 'This is nature.'

'Get out.'

Grandma put her hand over my face and pushed me backward.

'I have to pee,' I protested.

I could see him there, through her fingers, standing in front of the mirror. Something that looked like a dishevelled furry animal was strapped to his legs and dangled there, corpse-like.

'Grandpa's got a dead squirrel hanging off him,' I wailed.

She shut the door behind her, truncating the image of my startled grandfather wrapping a towel around his waist.

'Haven't you learned to knock?'

'Are you going to cut it off?'

'What?'

'With the chainsaw.' The chainsaw still lived in the bathtub.

She looked at me as if I were Lucifer.

'You're going to say extra prayers tonight, mark my words.'

'Why does he have a dead squirrel strung around his stomach?'

'You listen to me,' she commanded. 'Your grandfather's not well.' She lowered her voice to a mere hum. 'He might have an internal problem. So I'm checking to make sure he's all right Down There.' And she pointed toward her own abdomen.

'You go back to your room and wait until we're finished.' She shoved me toward the staircase.

That was the start of the first cancer.

I woke up when I heard the door slam shut. A few minutes later I heard a crunch.

'JesusMary'nJoseph! – the phone,' Grandma wailed.

He was slumped against the wall. She stood with her back toward me. The phone looked at us accusingly with its two black eyes, its single lopsided ear. Our telephone was a wooden box with two bells and a cranking handle, just like the ones Alexander Graham Bell used. It would never work again.

I heard the splinter of wood on flesh again.

'That's for every Jesus hour you spend talking to your goddamn sisters,' he shouted, his voice rough as a chainsaw that hadn't been properly greased.

'Sandy!'

He lunged at the wall by the phone. The cabinet surrounding it was made of plywood, so it crumpled effortlessly beneath his solid fist. His hand went right through the wall, exposing the maze of complex telephone wires that fed the old contraption. They dangled there, hanging limply like the tattered veins and arteries of the corpses I'd seen being taken away from car crashes on the Trans–Canada Highway.

A few minutes later he stood against the wall, his head in his hands, the tears welling out from between the thick calloused fingers. My grandmother and I stood silent, looking at the hole, caught in the thick immovable air that follows momentary disasters.

She saw me out of the corner of her eye.

'For Christ's sake, think of Morag,' she said.

He looked up, clear-eyed, at her and then at me.

'Yes,' he mumbled. 'Yes.'

She could stop him in his tracks just by mentioning my name.

I knew where I would find her – at the far end of the table, staring out into the night at the shadows the moon cast on the silvery limbs of the old apple tree. She spoke to me without even looking around.

'You're a fool for siding with your grandfather. He's trying to buy your affections and telling you he'll always love you and the rest of that bullshit. He just wants a sparring partner. Someone to take on the rest of the world with. He doesn't care whether it's you or Joe Blow.'

Her voice had that hard, metallic tone, at once smug and broken.

'And you're stupid enough to fall for this.'

'You're always saying nasty things.'

'Who?' She finally turned around from the window. She looked at me, surprised, as if she hadn't been speaking to me at all.

'You and Maryanne and Jessie. All you do is say bad things about other people.'

'That's not true. We often say good things. They might just sound bad because they're too sophisticated for you. All you understand is black and white.'

'That's not true.'

'It is so.'

'I don't take sides, Grandma.'

'Oh don't you now?' she cawed, just like the crows by the brook in the afternoon.

'You will,' she turned to me, clear-eyed, triumphant. 'Just you wait and see.'

My grandmother buries her independence of mind under a compost heap of certainties, each fermenting its own truth. She is virile and demure at the same time. When she is angry she is like an irritated snake, she seems to say: *I will rise like a cobra and seize control. I will protect my children in my hood*, she says, spitting venom. She does not know that the family is a very effective trap. It is a cell lined with thick warm buffalo skins and suffused with the smell of heated milk in winter. It is meant to comfort and of course she does not question the contiguous, continuing life of this family in which she is trapped, or of all families: breeding, becoming old; the drama of it all, visceral and embarrassing. The days that blend into one another for over thirty years have their own integrity, one handing over meaning to the next, like a baton passed in a relay race.

The family: a multi-generational saga of accident masquerading as a traceable series of events and associations, virtually without interest for all except those who are involved. The family: an epic of banalities.

In school I spent all my time looking at maps, particularly the strange time map we had on the wall, the one that had a black line that moved with the night as it encroached on the planet. It was made of ink or mercury, this substance. We could see the night creeping across or releasing the world hour by hour, like a black snake, coursing through the Carolinas, slithering on to the Blue Whale shape of Cuba, entering the irregular chain of isthmus countries as it curled around Puerto Cabezas, then to Easter Island and across to the reverse-image night on the other side of the world.

I learned, for instance, for the first time that we hardly ever inhabited the same night. Hers was the black southern night, the light bleeding from her cucumber sky suddenly, six hours ahead of our night, which came rumbling down from the Arctic. When she was in light, we were in dark. When we were on the ascendant, she was going down. Dawn catapulted her into a reality so different; the light milk, the air a woven mat of smells.

There was that night between us. Travelling far above her, on the great dark velvet of the continent, past Conrad's black viscous rivers of the Congo, over the biting sands of the Sahara, across a warm, metallic ocean, to where the tips of pines pierced the northern sky.

To our island, lost like Mauritius, teetering on the continental shelf in an unfriendly sea.

TEN

THE faded green linoleum on the kitchen floor was in need of a wash, the sheer curtains yellowed from cigarette smoke. The dishes were piled high in the dark pantry. Dan's wife had died young of cancer three years ago, and he was alone with the faded magazine pictures of the island that hung inexpertly framed on the wall, beside his certificates of chiefdom from the First Nations Association.

'Listen to this, Sandy.' Dan set down his beer bottle on the table and turned back to the book open on his knees. ' "Number twelve of the Trickster Cycle," ' he read aloud. ' "Dancing Ducks and Talking Anus. Number fourteen: Trickster Burns Anus and Eats His own Intestines. Number fifteen: Penis Placed in box. Number sixteen: Penis Sent Across Water." Isn't that something?' Dan looked up and grinned.

'Those guys sure had a strange sense of humour. The thing about Penis sent across the water – ' he added. 'There's a Micmac one just like that, where this poor guy named Panther loses his member 'cause there are these women across a river, and he wants to, you know ...' He glanced over toward me in the corner of the kitchen where I was playing dominoes by the stove.

'Hmm,' Dan cleared his throat. 'So he sends it across the water on the edge of a stick and it gets eaten by a fish. Terrifying, eh?'

'What's a penis?' I called.

Dan looked up from his book, his glasses slipping down on his nose, making him look like a schoolteacher. 'Oh, it's a small animal. We use it as bait for fish,' he improvised.

'Like a worm?' I asked. I had dug up worms for my grandfather's bait can. I liked pulling them out of the ground.

'Yeah, that's right,' Dan called.

'Er, Dan,' my grandfather mumbled. 'I don't think Morag should be listening to this.'

I looked up at them and smiled.

'Oh it's all right,' Dan soothed. 'She doesn't know what it means. Leave her be.'

'Yeah,' I said to Grandpa, 'leave me be.'

'You just watch yourself,' he barked.

'It's from the Winnebago, a tribe out West somewhere,' Dan continued, turning back to his book. 'I found it in this old book of my Dad's. It's part of the Trickster stuff I was telling you about. It's a series of stories they use to explain the world.'

'Pretty fuckin' strange world.' My grandfather plucked a cigarette from his breast pocket. 'What's this Trickster character anyway?'

'He's just a troublemaker,' Dan explained as my grandfather lit up. 'Most of the peoples have stories that feature some kind of Trickster or other. He's not really human. In the Micmac tales he's usually called Gluskap. He's the embodiment of chaos. He's there to explain the things that can't be explained. That's why he comes up in so many of the stories of different peoples. Apparently some anthropologist collected the entire Winnebago cycle. What a Jesus lot of work.' Dan took a swig of his beer.

'And listen: it gets weirder.' He wet his index finger and turned the page. ' "Trickster changed into woman," ' he read. ' "Trickster marries chief's son." Now this is a good one,' he grinned. ' "Trickster and the Laxative Bulb." And number twenty-four is called "Trickster Falls in His Own Excrement".'

'Wait a minute. The *laxative bulb*?' Grandpa chuckled. 'That's as good as the talking anus. I wonder, what do you supposed that anus was talking about anyway?'

'I imagine it said "shit" a lot.'

They both laughed until they had to reach for their respective handkerchiefs. 'And I always thought *Winnebago* was a make of camper van.' Grandpa dabbed the corners of his eyes and then started laughing again, so hard that he actually fell out of his chair.

I ran over to him. I thought he was drunk and had gone mad again. He lay on the floor, shuddering and twitching like a lizard. I looked up at Dan, wild-eyed.

'Don't you worry, Morag.' Dan came over to us, still laughing himself. 'He's as sober as a weasel. He'll get you home all right, I promise.'

Once a week we drove to the reserve. We toured the oyster pens, walking on thin wooden planks in between the beds, the gentle carbonized sound of oysters breeding bubbling on either side. Then we went to the restaurant, where we ate Lookineegun bread, Middle-Eastern in flavour and gently crusted, like a toasted pitta bread on the outside, but soft and doughy inside. If it was springtime we had Malagawatch eel with Fiddleheads, a fern which has to be picked by experienced hands, otherwise they are highly toxic; a few eaten at the wrong time can kill a grown man.

Moose was on the menu in season, but they had not served caribou in years. The caribou were all but gone now; the moose scarce. Even the bald eagles, which had once circled the air with the abundance of crows, were endangered. These ferocious predators, the story went, could hook a child in their claws. There were a few who still nested across from our house; we could pick them out easily even without a pair of binoculars, their white forms twirling against the mountain, riding the thermals. They had always lived there, their minds no doubt locked in a different time when we people were only trout and our houses salmon; when the lake was inhabited by gold and surrounded the green tweed of the forests, when this island and its abundance was monumental and without end.

★ ★ ★

We sailed along the highway on the way home that night, taking the turns too fast, cutting off the corners. It had snowed the week before and there were patches of thin ice on the road, hidden by fallen leaves mashed together by rain and frost.

There was a thump beneath the wheels.

'Shit.'

He was slowing down, eyes glued to the rear-view mirror. He stopped just below the crest of the hill, and pulled over onto the shoulder.

'What is it?'

'I dunno. Rabbit or a fox.' He reached above the visor for cigarette before getting out of the car.

'Are you comin' or not?' He held the door open barely long enough for me to scramble out onto the highway. There was no traffic. We walked down the hill a quarter mile to where we thought we had hit the animal. And there, in the middle of the road, was a smallish, scattered shape. A thin rivulet of dark liquid seeped from the body down the slope of the asphalt.

'Fox,' he grunted. 'I'll go back to the car and get some gloves. Never know what diseases these things carry. You stay here and get out of the way if you hear a car coming.' He loped off up the hill to the car, and I was left with the fox. It wore a grimace, and I could see its teeth glinting slightly, picking up the light from the overhead highway lamp a mile down the road. Its retracted gums gave it a vicious, agonized look. Its eyes were open, and looking right at me. In their pools was such an expression of pain and bewilderment, or sheer terror dulled by agony, that I wanted sit down and cry. Then its eyes shifted slightly, and I saw its expression of pure fear distilled into pain. Its muzzle twitched.

I screamed. 'It's alive.' I began to cry. 'It's alive. Please kill it, Grandpa.'

He came running down the hill.

'What the devil's the matter with you?'

I crouched on the highway shoulder, my hands covering my face.

'I know it's alive. I'm going to put it out of its misery. Now go back to the car and get in and stay there.'

He carried a big stick. The dull sound of a crunch came from behind me. I clambered into the car on the driver's side and lay with my face down on the passenger seat. After a moment I began to feel as though I was moving, a kind of dizziness. I sat up and looked out the rear window, and saw that he was coming closer.

The car was rolling down the hill, backward. Behind me I could see his back, bending over, about to pick up the fox and drag it over into the ditch.

I dived for the brakes. I clapped both hands on a thin pedal which gave way easily. Nothing happened. I switched from the pedal I had hit to the other two square pedals, placed a hand on either of them and pressed down. I heard a screech, and then a thud, like when we hit the fox. My head was thrust between the brake and the clutch, and my feet and legs were stuck up on the driver's seat. This was the position he found me in, when he opened the door.

'What the Jesus happened?' He plucked me out of my hole like a piece of lint, and set me on the roadside. The car began immediately to roll back again, and he dived into the driver's seat and tramped down on the brake. But one wheel had already gone over the edge of the bank.

'Holy fuck, you knocked it out of first,' he yelled, as the car's rear end careened into the ditch.

We stood there, a few minutes later, looking at the lopsided car.

'Christ, I don't think I can get that out myself.' He wiped the sweat from his forehead. 'Here, blow your nose.' He held the handkerchief over my nose. 'Blow! That's a good girl. I'll have to get Grant to tow me out tomorrow.'

He looked over his shoulder down the steep embankment. 'Another foot and I would've had her.'

He looked down at me, his face screwed up in the same way it did when he was angry, but sober. Had he been drunk, his face would have been slack as an old bloodhound's.

'We could've both been killed.'

He clambered down the bank and carefully opened the back door of the tilting car. He fetched a blanket and his jacket from the back seat.

He handed me the blanket and swung into the jacket. 'Put this around you, we'll have to wait for a lift.' And then he reached down, picked me up, and held me tight to his chest, so tight I couldn't breathe.

'I'm suffocating,' I cried.

'Shut up,' he said, but he drew me away from his chest. When I looked up at his face I could see neat rivulets, little wet creases, on his face.

'I don't know what I'd do if anything ever happened to you,' he sobbed, and then he plunked me down on the gravel while he dug in his shirt pocket for his hanky. I clung to his leg. He shook me off, only to crouch down beside me and take hold of my shoulders.

'Look at me,' he commanded. 'You know I never had no father, just like you?'

'You're my father.'

'I'm not,' he snapped. 'You know that. And that my mother went off on me, just like yours did? I'm talking about your mother. Your mother,' he repeated, shaking me.

'Get off,' I complained.

'We're the same, you and me.' He stood up to his full height. 'Nobody wants us, and nobody ever will. I'm going to tell you something now, and I want you to remember it.' He shook my shoulders a little, and I forgot about the cold.

'Never trust anyone.'

'Not even my friends?'

'Especially not your friends. You'll understand when you get older,' he said. 'You'll understand why I love you like nobody else. I'm alone in this world, and so are you.'

He turned his profile to me and lit a cigarette. The light of the overhead lamp about a mile down the road shone in his eye and against his glossy black hair. He thrust his hands in the pockets of his old leather jacket and I drew my blanket around my shoulders. We stood there on the roadside for an hour that night, waiting to flag down a passing car.

ELEVEN

'CHRISTMAS Ceilidh' poured from the radio, broadcast by the CBC in Sydney. It was nighttime in the kitchen of mundanity and euphoria. Maryanne and Jessie's kitchen was alternately the scene of raucous parties or excruciating stasis. More often they sat there, the two of them, smoking up forests of tobacco between them, one leg tucked underneath their bottoms, slowly disintegrating but strangely sustained by the mild rigors of their own comedy routine. They leapt up from their chairs in tandem and crashed into each other in their haste to get to the window, where they would twitch like brides as they watched the Dodge Pinto or Vega or some other antediluvian 70s car disappear around the bend. *Was that Annie? What's she doing going to town?* Between them they single-handedly upheld the stereotype of rural nosiness.

Maryanne and Jessie sat back down heavily. Just then the dog came bounding in, and they all nearly jumped off their chairs.

'How the hell did she get here?' Maryanne asked.

'He must have brought her.' Jessie lit her cigarette and cast a wary eye to the door.

'I didn't hear the car pull in.'

'I thought I heard something.'

'He must be just coming in now.'

'Yes, that's him,' my grandmother said. 'I can hear the door opening.'

They all strained their ears in the direction of the front door.

Then they braced themselves for his arrival.

The night before, 23 December, we were packing up to go to Maryanne and Jessie's for Christmas. The only thing I wanted to take was the dog, who would be my only sane and sober company for at least a week.

'You're not taking that mangy animal,' he said.

'She not MANGY,' I yelled at him.

My grandmother came to my defence. 'We're taking her if I have to walk all the way up there and carry her myself.'

So he had driven off into the night, leaving her, the dog, and me in the Big House. It was one of those sudden momentary disasters that seemed to swirl around my grandfather, but would mysteriously land on us, sparing him.

'Does this mean we'll have no Christmas?' I asked.

'It certainly doesn't.' My grandmother's mouth was set. She rang up her friend Rita, who came down in her pickup truck.

'Morag'll have to hold the dog in the back,' she said.

Getting a ride in the back of a pickup truck, especially on the highway, was the best possible thing that could happen. I sat on a blanket with my back hard up against the cab, watching the highway streak away behind us. The wind plastered the dog's ears right back against her head. The night was clear and cold and the stars very bright. We slipstreamed through the night and I gazed contentedly at the sky, drinking the cold wind, which hurt my nostrils. I could make out the Big Dipper, and the cluster of mottled light that was the Milky Way.

My grandfather did not arrive at Maryanne and Jessie's until around midnight. Aunt Jessie had to go downstairs to the cold and dark store to let him in because Grandma was afraid.

'There are ghosts down there,' she explained.

'The only ghost is your husband, Christine,' scoffed Jessie, putting on her dressing gown, 'who is in fact more like what I'd call a pre-corpse.'

*   *   *

73

Everything changed as soon as he arrived. He put down his fiddle and went back to the car to get his guitar and his mouth organ harness and small amps. Rum bottles were being lined up and the sandwiches spread out on the kitchen table. He had only put down his case and rolled a cigarette, but already he was the life of the party.

'How's tricks, Sandy?' the men went up to shake his hand.

Outside, headlights swept along the unlit tree-lined road and arced into the driveway, where sounds of laughter were punctuated by the slamming of car doors. By midnight there would be over a hundred people in their kitchen.

My grandmother tied ribbon around oranges that had been pierced with cloves.

'What's that?' I took a whiff of their combined scent, both sweet and acrid. It smelled like the images that graced our walls during the slide shows.

'This is to make the kitchen smell nice,' my grandmother explained. 'There'll be so many people in here sweating we need some deodorizer.'

I looked at the oranges. Their skin had puckered and dried up like an old woman's face where the cloves had been pushed through. Only the brown heads showed, sticking up through the skin. They looked like exotic pincushions.

People kept pouring through the door; perfume and alcohol mixed with the smell of seared oranges.

'Let's have a few Angus Chisholm tunes, Sandy,' someone joked. 'Just so we can get our blood pressure up.'

'You wait, b'y,' he laughed. 'I'll have you in the hospital by the morning.'

I wasn't going to get any sense out of anyone from this point onward, so I took the dog and went outside. The night was impenetrable, transfigured by the vicissitudes of our latitude. The dark and the minus twenty cold gave the combined effect of walking through an abattoir freezer swathed in felt. The dog and I stood still, our breath hovering in front of us in great gauzy clumps. Across the gut of the Bras d'or lakes the lights of Big Harbour reflected the calm winter-black water of the lake, unruffled by waves, a giant oily slick. It would be seven hours before the weak dawn light, freed from the black mercury snake of the nightmap at school, would advance on the snow, its purple creeping into crevices between the snowdrifts like the sun-shadows of stones. It must nearly be dawn for her, I thought. What would it be to wake on Christmas morning in Africa?

I wiped a hole in the frost and condensation on the foggy kitchen window and watched them from outside. Grandpa and his half-brother Alastair sat on the edges of their chairs in the corner of the kitchen, sweat like grease on their foreheads as they launched into the swift arpeggio leading into the medley of Angus Chisholm tunes they always played as a climax. They sat with a forty-ouncer of dark rum between them, already half empty, and the small microphone dripping condensation with their combined heat. A black wet cowlick fell over Grandpa's forehead, and drops of sweat ran delicately down the length of his nose. He did not even lift his face to receive the applause after each number. His pose was rapturous, so that he might have been praying.

When he played he seemed to have been transported to some exalted place of pure feeling. What lived there, though, was an old, sepia-tinted emotion, with pictures hung upside down in an archive of his past which he maintained for his own viewing pleasure, or more likely pain. And in the continuous film of his past were the scenes that had made him the man I knew so much later, when he was nearly finished, although he was a young man, really, a man of only forty-eight or forty-nine. But by then he had exhausted the intoxicating continuous fluid dream of becoming.

'Whatsa matter, Alexander Neil,' the other boys sneered, taunting him by using his full name, the grand one his mother had given him.

Every day, no matter how cold, he would hitch up the draught horses to the sleigh, and drive his sisters and Alastair to school.

'Can't come to school? Why don't ya come in for a few minutes, warm yer arse. Whatsa matter, Alexander Neil? Can't read, can't write and can't speak,' they chanted.

'And yer mother's a whore.'

Alexander put his frozen hands back on the reins and giddy-upped the giant Percheron horses into a trot, pulling away smoothly in the fresh-fallen snow, leaving his abusers straggling behind him like confused sheep. Back at the house, alone, he lit a small fire, just enough to keep himself warm in the kitchen.

One night, the kitchen caught fire. If his mother had been there she would have seen him running like a madman from the shed to the waterpump to the brook, buckets sloshing half their contents into the snow. At one point he had to get out a ladder and pour the freezing water on the roof. His dungarees flapped in the wind. It was the middle of January and there he was with a nightshirt and a pair of denims on, his feet bare in his boots. He wouldn't warm himself up by the kitchen fire after he put it out because he was too scared of seeing flames. He saved his sisters and his half-brother and himself that night, and the house. He couldn't save his mother, because she was not there.

In the spring, the first iceberg drifting down from New-foundland signalled the return of his mother.

'Where's my father?' he asked her. And she slapped him. Other times she said, 'Your father left me and now he's living in sin in Illinois or Indiana. He might as well have gone to hell.' She spat on the ground. 'That's what I think of your fuckin' father.' She took him by the scruff of his neck and forced him to look at her spit, sizzling through the snow. It was she who schooled him in the complex choreography of manipulations.

There is a photograph, one in which he stands behind his sisters and Alastair, his half-brother, his arms around all their shoulders. He wears dusty overalls and no shoes. It was the third summer of the Great Depression. He looks right at the camera, a pinched, John Steinbeck face, not yet marked by the slightly puckered skin and sparse eyebrows that came later as a result of the fire in the tank. His face is a study of calculation: *Who can I trust? Who has done this to me? Who can I hurt?*

It was his mother, of course. But he couldn't hurt her. He would have to wait until he had a wife.

The last thing he sang that Christmas Eve was Sweeney's Gaelic '*Salm an Fhiarainn*', the Psalm of the Land. He was the soloist; the company the chorus. He sang as if he were a priest leading a congregation on Barra, South Uist, Eriskay, Benbecula; one of those tripping-syllable places from which we had come.

It was a reedy, piped sound, tribal, minor-keyed, and Middle-Eastern in its wailing. It spoke of a bone-chilling devotion come galloping out of the desert, drifting across the velvet skin of Asia, carrying the historical migration of the Celts on its back. There was something animal about his singing; as if it were poised between flux and the sound made in the throats of animals, originating in a lower cortex, a dumb language centre built not to carry meaning but rather the sounds of alarm and orgasm.

Their tonal progression wound melancholy and adoration around one another like the ropes used to secure masts' riggings. The sounds listed to the side, more than forty-five degrees, capsizing in a small trough, getting buried in throats before they bobbed up again, perfect and preserved but changed, compositionally, in their brush with ending. In their delivery nothing was held back but something was left behind, clanking, at the bottom of the barrel of emotion. something hard, like an old rusted gun. It resonated in there, with the mute sadness of animals when they smell their own death.

Sound, and what he did to it. So that I knew what to believe in (him, her, the land, our language, music, our future together fanning out in front of us, uncatastrophic and without end).

So that I knew what was real.

* * *

The kitchen looked as though it had been hit by a tornado. It was five in the morning and I was upstairs, my moon face squished against the iron slats of the register grille, peering down into the survivors of the party, who sat shipwrecked in the kitchen.

'What are you going to do with Morag? She's taking after her grandfather more each day.'

'Morag's no more like her grandfather than the Pope.' I heard my grandmother's voice, clear and strong above the din. 'He's just got her convinced that there's some cosmic relationship between them. She follows him around like a little dog. Out into the woods; trapping, fishing, shooting. Can you imagine it? At her age, learning to shoot? He takes her to the homes of all his cronies while they drink. He carts her around as if she were a goddamned mascot. And she loves him for it. Me? I go out to the clothesline. How can I compete with him?'

'You know she'd be better off with her mother,' Maryanne said. 'Seriously, Christine,' Maryanne's voice came through the register. 'What kind of an education is that for a girl? She'll grow up to be a tomboy. She'll be queer. She spends all her time with that dog. She doesn't know any other children.'

'Her mother will take her to the city,' Jessie echoed. 'She can go to a good school there, take drawing classes, take ballet.'

Plates and glasses clattered on the counter, and the water faucet was turned on and off, so that I missed most of what they said next.

'You've got to think of her future,' I heard Jessie say. 'She's going to need a good education if she's going to get anywhere.'

'Education only makes you sad,' Grandma said. 'The more you know, the sadder you get. Look at her grandfather.'

'He isn't educated,' said Maryanne.

'He is, after a fashion. He's travelled.'

'What's Bridget doing out there anyway?' Jessie asked.

'Still studying,' my grandmother said. 'I didn't know studying took so long.'

Maryanne put her glass down with a rap. 'Well, that's the way it is with all the young people, isn't it? They're always after studying something these days. They wouldn't want to be getting a job, now would they?'

'You mean they'd rather be sitting on their arses like us,' Jessie drawled.

'Well, she didn't have to go so far away to study, did she?' Maryanne retorted. 'There's plenty of things to study right here at home.'

'Like how to pick up your pogey check?' Jessie scoffed. 'They teach you to do that pretty good here.'

There was a long silence.

'What're you going to do, Christine?' Maryanne asked.

'I don't know,' my grandmother said. 'We'll wait until the spring. She may not want her.'

'Who won't want who?' asked Maryanne. 'The child or her mother?'

'Neither, maybe. It doesn't matter,' she said, getting up from the rocking chair, which creaked in protest. 'I'm her mother now.'

I looked up from the grille, feeling slightly sick. And what I looked up into was the face of my grandfather, standing above me in his pyjamas, and staring at me in a way I had never seen him do before. His face was like a hypnotist's, concentrated and focused. He seemed to be deciding something.

He looked at me a long time. Then he whispered to me, 'Is that what you want to do? Go with your mother? She doesn't love you, you know. Or she never would have left you.'

'What are you talking about?' I whispered back.

He didn't answer. He only said: 'Go to your bed now.'

And then he went back to his room, his thick woollen socks and long flannel nightshirt swishing against the carpet and then disappearing as he closed the door.

'Is Bridget a missionary?'

'Where in the name of God did you get that idea?' My grandmother nearly choked on her tea.

He sat eating, unconcerned, at the opposite end of the kitchen table.

'Missionaries go to Africa,' I reasoned.

'Catholics do not have missionaries,' she said firmly. 'And certainly not women ones.'

'What is she?'

'She's . . .' my grandmother began.

'Do you want any Christmas presents or not?' he growled.

The heat. Her fan hums noisily, some metal part scrapes against its counterpart every two or three rotations. She goes to sleep under her mosquito net, its white tulle making her bed a bridal chamber. A centipede lurks in the corner of her ceiling. It seems as big as her sun hat. Windless night, insects and the hissing of rain. The dark canvas of black as it is tacked suddenly across the sky, the sun going down like a bloodied meteor, leaving her stranded in its inky wake.

WINTER

TWELVE

HE ran past me as I stood stupid in the doorway of my room, rubbing my eyes. He stopped, turned on a dime, came back, and snagged me like he would bait a fish hook. Soon I was running too.

He went upstairs to get his rifle.

'There's a fire at the Campbells',' he said in between breaths, pointing out of the window. From the sea-facing window of the Big House we saw the black sky, scorched and toxic with flames and smoke. Through the gusts of wind the flames rattled into sight, and then disappeared behind another white blanket of driven snow.

'Get your snowsuit on,' he called over his shoulder.

'You're not taking her,' she said flatly.

'I Jesus well am.' He looked up at her sharply, tying the laces on his snowboots. 'I need some company.'

'It's two in the morning,' she called, but we were already out the door.

We put our snowshoes on in front of the shed. I coaxed the dog out from her house and we headed off through the woods. I followed the arc of light from my flashlight as it shone on the tails of my grandfather's advancing snowshoes. Beneath the tall pines the roar of the wind and the sea was strangely distant, the driving snow muffled.

When we reached the woods we could see the orange light again through the trees. Then we emerged, slipping and sliding downhill to the shore, where the cabin stood burning. Just as we arrived, glass blew out from one of the upstairs rooms. The forest cracked on the back of the blizzard, and more of the upstairs windows blew out. I looked across at my grandfather's face.

'Jesus,' he said. 'I sure hate fire.'

I saw apprehension scramble over his face like a crab. Then it was gone and he disappeared into the red and black mess of the burning cabin.

The next morning the dog and I sat in the bathtub, which had landed in the driveway and was now full of snow. I made snowballs and the dog licked at the sides of the tub. Flurries were still floating down, but the storm had moved out to sea. My grandfather was picking through the blackened wreck that surrounded the chimney, the only part of the house standing, besides the bathtub.

'Got a saucer ... Got a doorknob,' he yelled to me. He held up the half-charred relics triumphantly, then stooped over again, trying to retrieve something of the old couple's lives.

The Campbells had slept in my grandparents' bed until the ambulance arrived from Sydney Mines. Mrs Campbell had been singed a little as my grandfather carried her out of the burning walls. Mr Campbell suffered from shock and mild hypothermia. My grandfather had dragged them both uphill to the Big House on my play sled. They were huddled in heavy blankets, and I had to push them from behind, my hands on their trembling backs, my heels dug into the snow, as we went uphill back to the house. Ahead of me in the night, I watched my grandfather's stooped back, the sled rope taut around his chest, the rifle slung over his shoulder, his eyes on the dog who traced our path back through the woods. He turned to look behind him from time to time, to me, where I trudged behind, thinking that I would follow him, as I followed him now, over our land, over our years on the island, forever.

✱   ✱   ✱

My grandmother came running out to the shed.

'Sandy,' she gasped. 'You've got to come in the house right now.'

He looked at her, his thumb still in the middle of measuring the thickness of the plank.

'In a second,' he mumbled.

'*Right now,*' she said.

He took off his gloves and left them on the plank.

She led him by the arm to his mother's bedroom and opened the door. We all peered in.

There she was, on the bed, sleeping. Her feet were encased in gold slippers, just like Cinderella.

'She's sleeping,' he shrugged. 'So what?'

My grandmother pointed to the bedside table. On it was a bottle of pills; or rather a bottle. The pills were gone.

'Her sleeping pills,' he gasped, and lunged for the bottle.

'What are we going to do?' Grandma nearly cried.

'Ambulance.'

It was cold in the room. Then I saw that the window was open.

'The window's open.' My grandmother was already halfway out the door.

'Go away, Morag. Go to your room.'

Then she stopped in front of me, so that I crashed into her.

'What is it?' he asked.

My grandmother went back into the room and peered again at the open window. In a flash she had her boots on and was outside. I watched her from my great-grandmother's room. She looked at the snow underneath the sash. It was pock-marked, as if icicles had fallen from the eaves. And in the bottom of the little holes was the colour blue. She fingered one out, and held it up in her hand. A blue capsule.

Beside me, something stirred. It was Great-Grandma.

'Okay, Mama,' I heard him say.

She was off the bed like a cat and had the window open in a

second. Half her body was out. Just her legs and her gold slippers fluttered in the air as she tried to propel herself head first out into the snow. My grandfather caught her around the waist. Great-Grandma's dress got hitched up and we could see her underwear.

'Let go of me,' she screamed. She scrabbled and scrabbled but my grandfather was too strong and he hauled her in and sat her back on the bed.

She sat there, arms folded, thunderheads on her face.

'What a production,' my grandmother said, disgusted. She walked away and I heard the front door slam. My grandfather retrieved the gold slippers from where they had been kicked off and gently put them back on his mother's feet. There was something so grotesque about this gesture of supplication, to see him bent down in front of his own mother, replacing her gold slippers, that I turned away and went upstairs to my room.

That was the bizarre thing about it all: she had tried to jump out of a window that was only two feet above the ground. The rest of us slept on the second floor: my great-grandmother's bedroom was downstairs, next to the living room.

THIRTEEN

HE came in the house and the cold followed like a dog at his heels.

'What's the matter with you?' he asked, before he had even shut the door behind him.

I felt the draught like a snake against my leg. My eyes followed his every movement as if I were tracking an animal.

'I said what the name of Jesus is the matter with YOU?' He lunged toward me.

The copper pots hanging on hooks above the sink rattled.

My eyes went away to somewhere inside my head. He could smell my absence. He turned toward his wife.

'Where's my fuckin' dinner?'

She folded her arms across her chest.

'On the table.'

She was strong, he knew that. He had to build himself up to a point where a freight train could not stop him to get past her thick arms. He knew the walls of her stomach were thin with wanting no more children. He kicked her there.

I retreated to a far corner, a single word floating like a diamond in my head: *Carnivore.*

He whipped around toward me, one of the many heads of the Hydra.

'What are you doing there?' He came toward me.

What was I doing?

'Cowering in the corner?' he teased.

Behind him my grandmother rose from the floor like Jesus and dusted herself off.

'Come on now,' he said, proffering his hand. 'What are you doing there?' His tone softened to the one he used for coaxing recalcitrant animals.

The hand came toward me. I had seen that hand release animals, broken and frozen, from steel traps.

'Come on darlin'. Come out of there.' His voice was smoothed and oiled. 'We're going to have supper.'

The hand came closer and closer.

I bit it.

The glass cracked as she hit the window. He took two steps toward her while she took two steps back. He gave her a left hook – he had told me this was his best punch – and sent her reeling backwards. She fell into the swivel chair, and swivelled toward the wall. I saw her glasses fly off her face. She sat in the chair, feeling blindly on the floor with her hands, trying to find them. I knelt down and retrieved them from where they had landed underneath the chair, dusted them off and handed them over.

'Thank you,' she mumbled. She put them on and looked at me. 'You should be in bed.'

He advanced on her again. He threw his arms out wide on either side of himself, looking like the statue of Christ the Redeemer above Rio de Janeiro, and tried to embrace her.

'*Bitch*,' I heard him say to her, so soft it could have been loving.

She runs out of the house and is immediately plunged into snow. It is night, and she has no flashlight. The moon is rising over the tops of the tall eastern-facing pines. She wades her way through the drifts, which are rising with the east wind, and makes it to the top of the driveway, across the road, and up the road another mile, maybe. She knocks on the door of Archie and Mary, the nearest neighbours. I know what they say. They say: calm down, Christine. We'll go down to the house and talk to him. It can't be that bad.

And I'm in the house, so I know. I know what has happened to drive her out that door and I know that he is pacing back and forth across the worn green linoleum like a caged jaguar. I see the yellow, empty eyes and the spots that change colour in response to the rainforest gloom or light. I see him saying things to himself, over and over again. I see his knuckles itchy for contact with a surface. He is only harnessed hysteria behind a melting charm.

And then they are at the door. I see my grandfather turn around, and in that moment he changes completely, like an actor at an audition changing seamlessly from one character to the next.

'Hello, b'y,' he greets Archie, coming forward to shake his hand. 'Hello, Mary,' he says to the wife. 'Don't you have good colour for so far into winter.'

My grandmother trails in like a lost dog.

He closes the door solicitously behind her.

'How 'bout a toddy?' he grins at his guests, holding out the chair for Mary. 'What brings you down here on such a Jesus awful night?'

Archie looks confused. He and Mary exchange hesitant looks. His big man's fingers set to fumbling under the table.

'Christine thought it might be a good idea for us to come down and talk to you.'

My grandmother pulls herself out a chair and sits down at the table.

'About what?' my grandfather calls over his shoulder from the pantry, where he is fixing the toddies.

'You seem to be pretty upset tonight.'

'Me?' My grandfather shakes his head. 'No, I'm right as rain. How're you twos getting along anyway?'

And from there until several hours later when my grandfather is entertaining the company with a tune on the mouth organ, when they are all laughing and clapping and watching him as he seems to devour the music, sucking in and out on the instrument he loves, all his body bent in the effort of extracting sound from that one little reed – torso swaying and heaving, hands flapping to control the vibrato, feet miraculously keeping the two separate rhythms of the tune's times – in those few hours I watch my grandmother deflate, quietly, until she looks like a heap of old washing sitting on the kitchen floor, mauled by circumstance, waiting to be done.

The Big House is the Winter Palace. All around it, minus thirty and the snowdrifts approach like sentries.

Inside is the Snow Queen, shimmering in her woman's paleness.

There, too, is the suave Prince, so charming. He greets his guests, who have sometimes travelled far – in this case from the house across the highway, in fact – to receive his regal hospitality, which he obliges; calm, witty, joking; rolling cigarettes.

The Snow Queen sits, looking nervous, the guests think: look how she pushes her drink around like a chess piece. Look how she fingers her cigarette roll-up paper to shreds. And so pale.

She must not be well, they conclude, and lament the delicacy of women.

After he ushers the guests out the door, off into the howling night where the snowdrifts wait to check their passports, harass them a little, and then let them back into their own country; after he performs this gesture he turns, shuts the door behind him and looks at her, sitting at the table. She sits there, the Snow Queen, a blank screen for receiving his attention.

A mamba, a hyena, a dumb bear; he turns back into the feral scrabbling animal he is.

He turns on her.

Africa is a continent that is almost an island. Africa, where snakes coil, poised for their vertical flight through air toward the white neck of their prey. Where the green monkey ambles alongside the road, between the track and the ditch, and then breaks into a skip to gain momentum to climb the baobab tree. Where the lion wanders into your back yard and wakes you with a roar that travels up and down the rickety ladder of your spine. Africa, where the choir assembles to sing the Kyrie, praising God in their earth-hued, celestial percussion of voices.

Does God hear anything coming from that vast green-and-dust carpet, the thick muffler of sound, of the screams of the dying antelope and the grunts of the lion's loins? Perhaps God is deaf to that continent as he is deaf to this island.

In the morning he came into the kitchen, looking grey.

'Oh, God, my head hurts,' he moaned. 'I could use a cup of tea to get rid of this fog in my head. Oh, Jeeeesus . . .' he moaned.

My grandmother sat with a few icecubes wrapped in cheese-cloth, applying them to her bruised and swollen eye.

'Okay, Sandy. I'll get you a cup of tea.' She got up out of the chair, stiffly raising her frame. 'Hang on.'

When he had had his cup of tea he surveyed the damage around him.

'Christ, what a lot of mess I can make.' He looked at the overturned chairs, the smashed glass of the ashtray and the broken shelf that he had punched down. 'I saw some scenes of devastation in the War, but this is just something else.' He shook his head, his lips pressed flat together, then turned toward us, bright-faced.

'Why don't we just call it the Alcoholocaust?' he laughed.

FOURTEEN

W HEN her sisters came for a visit it was like being set upon by a two-headed invasive force. Maryanne and Jessie had been together so long that their boundaries had blurred. Their women's bodies bred the same expectations of the space around them, which moved away accordingly to accommodate their large breasts, the wide-sprung hips, the childless thighs. They needed everything to be just so: the white rum and 7-up had to be mixed to just the right proportions; the tea had to be brewed just right; they had had total control over every aspect of their environment for so long that even the slightest free radical could throw them into chaos. After they had been served their rum and tea I was allowed to sit with the three sisters in the kitchen, as long as I remained quiet.

'If I ever got my hands on him I'd show him a thing or two. What kind of man is he?'

'Are you talking about Grandpa?' I asked.

'No, I'm not,' she snapped.

'What kind of piece of trash leaves a young woman in that situation?' She turned to her sisters.

'It's all the rage these days,' Maryanne shrugged.

'Who're you talking about?' I asked.

'Never you mind,' she threw her head in my direction, as if I were the dog – not really there and, even if I was, I ought not to be understanding the English language.

She turned back to her sisters. 'He'd better learn to fear the day his path crosses mine.'

'It was years ago now, Christine, calm down,' Maryanne soothed. 'Morag doesn't need him. She's got you, too. She doesn't need her either, for that matter.'

'WHO ARE YOU TALKING ABOUT?' I screeched.

'That's it for you, young lady.' She hauled me off my feet by the scruff of my neck, the way she picked up kittens. 'Off to bed with you.'

'I don't want to go to bed,' I complained, kicking and bucking all the way up the stairs. 'It's only five o'clock.'

'Too bad,' she said.

'The wolfman will get me,' I wailed.

'Good for him.'

The wolfman lived in the woods, I was sure. Something malevolent was there. I was afraid to look out of the windows at night, fearing I'd come eye to eye with some large animal, half-man, half-beast. What would keep him from getting in the house?

There was a noise on the stairs.

'Who's that?' I panted.

'Calm down,' she snapped. 'It's just your grandfather.'

'She must have got caught in a trap.' He turned away from the window, where he was watching the snow start to come down in sheets.

The dog had not come home. A blizzard was coming in from the west. My grandfather went outside in the snow and stood on the step, listening against the howl of the wind.

He came back in. 'Get your snowboots on,' he commanded.

He went into the bedroom and came out with a gun.

'Don't cry now.' He put on his gloves. 'I'll only shoot her if there's nothing else to be done.'

The wind drove us into the trees and made us take mis-steps

in the snow. We went on, into the woods between the house and the sea.

'Let's go over there,' he said, looking up into the wind and turning his ear in the direction of the sea.

We were taking our breaths in great big gulps of ice-air. What seemed like hours later he shone the flashlight into the wood and there she was, whimpering, licking frantically at her paw and shivering.

Freeing his fingers from the warm enclave of his gloves, Grandpa made to disarm the trap. This was the most dangerous part, when the powerful spring could snap down on his fingers and cut them off, or it could damage the dog's paw so she would be crippled. He wrapped his thick woodsman's scarf around his fingers in a serpentine fashion, and held it over her paw. With his free hand he twisted wires and clicked clips.

Suddenly, with a snap I could hear over the noise of the wind, the trap came down on his protected hand. I was right up against him. He didn't even flinch. He gently extricated the dog and eased her into the folds of his jacket, where she shivered and sucked at the thick cloth of his lumberjack shirt. We walked home, face-down against the snow.

Normally he was rough with the dog. But that night he stayed awake all night, feeding her milk from the palm of his hand and heating up the waterbottle to keep her warm. He kept her injured paw away from the heat.

'Why aren't you warming up her paw?'

'With frostbite you've got to take care not to heat the body too quickly,' he explained. 'Or gangrene can set in, and then we would have to take her to the vet in town to have her leg amputated.'

'Can we go to town anyway?'

'Why do you want to go to town?'

'I don't know,' I said sullenly, and left the dog and my grand-father together by the stove and went to bed.

One of the first times I'd ever been to town had been to go

the vet in Sydney Mines. We had to have the dog spayed. As we approached the main intersection, I saw a bright purple Volkswagen beetle go by. Something made me look down at the road as we were stopped at a red light. Right beneath us, as the purple of the beetle flashed by, I saw a smear of white and red. Barely two feet away a white dog, a poodle, lay decapitated in the road. The head was several feet from the rest of its body. Its body was still moving. It was trying to run, the four legs jerking in every possible direction. The eye in the head was rolling wildly in all directions, trying to see what had happened. One side of its fur was white, the other red.

I was still hysterical when we reached the vet, who gave me a sedative with the needle he usually used on horses.

I was born in the winter. That was all anyone would tell me. I would be put out in a carriage on the veranda in the December cold and I would go to sleep happily, even though it was minus fifteen. I was born in the true north, where you can die on a cold night in the woods, lost and on unfamiliar ground, with no polestar to guide you. This landscape makes sense to me; it does not brook compromise, it takes no prisoners. Better that than a wet, seasonless place where the months are indistinguishable from one another except for the gradual lengthening or lassoing in of the daylight. This landscape and its seasons has to do with survival: with gritting your teeth and taking yourself through whatever you have to come through. Each winter is a death which has to be accepted and negotiated, knowing that resurrection is not a matter of virtue but of time. I am a Canadian. I survive every winter, so I know I can survive anything.

She got up and dusted herself off gingerly, as if she'd slipped and taken a fall by accident.

'God will be your judge,' she said. 'It's not up to me to judge you. And I won't hit back. So don't you think you're not doing wrong. Christ looked the other way.'

'And look where that got him,' he mumbled, his head between his hands. He scraped his chair backward and I jumped, thinking he was about to leave the room and catch me. Instead he went over to her, and knelt down in front of her.

'You wouldn't have thought this would be life, would you?'

'What would be life?' She cleaned her glasses on the hem of her shirt and put them back on her face, readjusting them carefully.

'This,' he gestured at the mottled brown and copper carpet.

'That?'

'Not the carpet. Jesus, you're literal minded,' he sighed. 'This.' He gestured more expansively.

'I never thought life would be one thing or the other. One thing's for sure, we're going to die and go to our maker.'

'But that's not much impetus for being alive,' he said.

'It's enough for me.'

'You're barely alive as it is. You're more at home being morose. You don't know the meaning of joy.'

'I'll know it when I see the Lord's face.'

'That might be a long time. It might be never. Look,' he implored, and spread the fingers on both his hands in front of her face. 'These are a surgeon's hands. That's what I could have been doing instead of cutting down trees.'

'What, a tree surgeon?' she scoffed. 'You're a sometime lumberjack. And last night you were going on about being a masseur and having a masseur's hands. Have your hands changed that much overnight?'

I heard him getting to his feet. He stood in my field of vision, rubbing his knees. 'You're a spiteful woman,' he sighed. 'You're full of spite because I had ambitions; I had hopes and I could see things that you could never see. Don't you realize we're all going to die some day?'

My grandmother sighed. 'The fact that we're all going to drop dead is no excuse for the way you carry on.'

He stepped back from her.

'And what kind of woman are you?' He hung his question in the air in the same way he would hang the carcass of an autumn pheasant upside down in the porch.

'Lonely,' she said, grasping it. 'I'm a lonely woman.'

The carnival at night: lights – purples, greens and oranges, the lurid colours of desire and euphoria – flashed as the death-defying rides whisked through the air in stupendous great ellipses. He was the carnival master, pulling the hydraulic lever that stopped the ferris wheel dead, so that it creaked in the night, the nervous occupants of the topmost car dangling in the chasm of air between them and the ground. In his own mind he was a good man, a fair man. (A fair ground man.) We approached the carnival grounds of his consciousness from a long way away, emerging out of the dark bushes by the nearby river, lured by the din of tinny music and the bright lights which promised euphoria. We walked hand in hand, mouths open, expectant. Then we leaped into a ferris wheel carriage and he wheeled us up and up. And then backward through the wild nights.

I once was blind
but now I see

Her patience was what he most exploited in order to continue with his chain of abuses. Because her patience was her last line of defence. And he played that patience like a twelve-string guitar; he teased it like a fierce small animal whose ferocity is a smokescreen for its natural timidity. When he won, and she lashed out, he was as pleased as the boy who had stuck his thumb in the pie. The twa corbies, crow and ravens in the pie. The nursery rhymes operated on the same principle as our landscape, the fusion of the beautifully pure and the unmistakably sinister. The light was returning from the south as it did every winter, spreading out, almost imperceptibly, the silk skirts of evening. The ravens sang, balanced on the telephone wire.

Amazing Grace
How sweet the sound
that saved a wretch
like me

She hummed, sitting on the edge of the bed, her head cradled between her hands. A loving embrace. Her head, a watermelon, a piece of fruit that could be smashed, if dropped in the right place. He was nowhere to be seen.

FIFTEEN

'GET dressed.'
He threw some clothes onto the bed. I rubbed my eyes and squinted at him.

'You heard me. We're going for a drive.'

We left the Big House with all the lights on. The dog whined in the doorway. I whined too.

'Leave that damn dog,' he said.

Grandma was at work. I started to scream and he shoved me in the back of the car. I hit the far door and passed out.

'We're driving to Mexico,' he said, when I came to a few minutes later. 'And then we'll get a boat to Australia. I've always wanted to go to Australia.' He grinned at me in the rear-view mirror. I was huddled on the back seat, slumped into a corner, trying to ignore the miles of pine trees that flew by the window.

'At least they got a decent climate out there,' he said. 'And I met some Australian chaps in the war – nice fellows. And those two girls I picked up hitchhiking and took up to the Buddhist monastery to meet the monks. We had a great time. I've got their addresses – we could probably stay with them.' He was always picking up hitchhikers.

'Hit the road, Jack, and don't you come back no more no more no more . . .' he sang in the front seat.

Ten hours later we topped at the Maine border and the American Duty Free where he bought four bottles of overproof navy rum.

99

'Can't get this in Canada. What a fuckin' poor excuse for a country. It's all them Protestant bastards. I bet they poke their wives through a hole in the sheet.' He stowed the bottles on the floor of the passenger seat in a paper bag where they rattled threateningly every time we hit a pothole.

We drove on the timber-lined highways of New Hampshire and northern Vermont. All day transport trucks screamed past. They moved like the big game animals on the plains of Zimbabwe in Bridget's pictures; clumsy but with a certain delicacy. Herds of them flashed their lights, beeped their horns and swore as their drivers looked down on my grandfather, hands tight at the helm of his tiny Chevette. In their midst he must have looked like a crazed Greenpeace campaigner, buzzing in his raft around the hulls of Norwegian whalers.

'I'm driving this way to avoid the toll highways.' He drew the lighter out of the dashboard and lit another cigarette.

We drove on progressively smaller roads until it seemed we were travelling on the asphalted equivalent of an ox-cart track. You had to pay money to drive on some American roads and he didn't agree with this in principle. He probably would have driven to Alaska to avoid paying thirty cents at the toll highways.

He stopped by the side of a lake. He got out and went to the trunk. The moon shone through a thin curtain of high cloud, underneath which raced thicker, bigger storm clouds, hurtling by at vampire-movie speed. When the moon was snuffed out we couldn't see a thing. He pulled the blades from out underneath the spare tyre.

'What are you doing?'

'Going skating.' Puffs of air rose from his mouth. When the moon darted out it shone on his hair, black as an oil slick and just as lustrous. He tied the skates onto his shoes.

'Why are you going skating?' It was close to midnight.

'Because I feel like it,' he snapped. 'I've been sitting down driving all goddamn day and I need some exercise.'

'Maybe the ice is too thin.'

'It's deep enough all right. How long do you think I've been alive? I know my frozen lakes. You just sit on that log and keep quiet.'

He was wearing black, his long black overcoat that split out at the back to look like a fancy livery costume; the kind nineteenth-century coach drivers used to wear. He put the skates on his feet and then disappeared off into the blackness.

The only sound was the cut of the blades, that strangely disturbing noise, ice-knives on his feet, like a scalpel slicing through flesh, rhythmic and metallic in his long, beautiful, practised skater's strokes. When the moon came out from behind its shroud I could see his figure gliding over the ice. His coat billowed out behind him so that he looked like a giant crow or magpie, a black bird flying just over the surface of something dangerous.

I stood at the side of the lake, stamping my feet and blowing hot air into my mittened hands, squinting into the darkness and willing the moon to reappear so I could see if he had fallen through yet. Would it sound like when the moose delicately step through the thin meniscus of ice in the November streams? Would he yell? I began to look around for suitable trees. In school we were shown films on how to save someone who had fallen through the ice without falling in yourself: we were instructed to extend a long branch, preferably of pliable and wet young wood, but strong, while standing well back from the hole. The victim would grasp it, and we would pull them to safety across the ice.

It was midnight in northern New Hampshire; we were in the middle of nowhere parked beside a frozen lake and he was skating. After a while I couldn't hear him at all anymore. He must have fallen in, I thought, or gone over to that foreign land, the one on the other side of the night.

'She's cute,' said the waitress in the gas station restaurant the next morning. She had a beehive hairdo and horn-rimmed glasses and looked like my grandmother.

'We're on our way to Cleveland,' he explained. The waitress wrinkled up her nose at the sound of Cleveland so that her glasses were shoved up right against her eyelashes.

'We've got relations there. We won't stay for long,' he finished.

Grandpa ordered coffee, but I wanted tea, like we had at home.

'You're not at home anymore, so you'll Jesus well drink what I drink.'

I studied the map on the placemats while I waited for my coffee. It showed the New England area, and mapped out all the interstates. I 95, New Jersey Turnpike, Stockbridge, Boston, Montpelier. The map stopped at Vermont.

'What's after Vermont?' I asked him.

'To tell you the truth I can't remember,' he said in wonderment. 'All these states down here, I don't know how they keep track of them.'

On the other side of Lake Champlain he started drinking. He pulled out a bottle from the brown paper sack he stowed underneath the passenger seat.

'What are you doing?'

'Just having a drink.' He raised the bottle to his lips.

'You're not supposed to drink and drive.' I shrank back into the seat.

'Don't you think I Jesus well know that?' he shouted at the rear-view mirror, where he could see me. I shimmied outside of its range and sank back in the corner. 'Don't you think I've been pulled on the side of the Jesus road often enough by the pigs? You know they even tried to take my licence away from me?' he raved. 'Jesus fuckin' pigs,' he muttered, all the way through the twisting Adirondack roads. Just before we left the secondary road to turn onto the Interstate, I felt the car lurch, hurtle sideways and then everything was topsy-turvy. We went down, all the way down to hell.

As it turned out we only went into the ditch. When we shuddered to a stop everything was very quiet and peaceful. I noticed that the birds were singing, which is something I hadn't been able to hear while we drove. I decided to move. I leant forward and said, 'Grandpa?'

He was slumped against the wheel. Blood came out of his nose and fell onto his pants. I put my fingers to his throat like we did when we took animals out of the traps. He was breathing.

Out on the side of the road, car after car went past me. I hadn't figured on this, because at home everybody stopped. But in the States they must have been afraid to, because the seven-year-old child at the side of the road could have been a decoy for a group of escaped convicts, or rapists. Finally someone pulled up.

'Lost, little girl?' A man with a thick moustache said to me in a long, drawling accent when he had rolled down the window. He had a small smile on his face, and a strange droopy look in his eyes.

'No . . .'

'Why don't you get in the car with me and I'll take you for a little ride?'

'Because my grandfather's in the ditch,' I gasped. 'I've got to get him to hospital. Can you take us?'

The man had jumped out of the car now, and was behaving less strangely. He walked over to the edge of the road and looked down.

'Jesus. You stay here,' he commanded. 'I'll radio the police. He shouldn't be moved.'

In the hospital the police asked him where we were going.

'Mexico,' he mumbled.

'Izatso?' said the bigger of the two twin policemen.

'We're going to Cleveland to visit his father,' I told them. They lost interest and then they left, gone to the next suspicious car crash.

'Australia,' my grandfather snarled when they had left. 'We're going to Australia. Mexico's just a stopover.'

He looked confused. Suddenly he took stock of his position, which was prone.

'Where the Jesus am I?' he asked, looking around the room, from the television to the orderly to me. Then he put his head in his hands and cried.

'Don't cry.' I put my hand on his back as he did with me when I was upset. I could see the tears popping out from between his fingers, just like the water escaped when Grandma put clothes through the wringer in the washing machine.

'Don't cry, please.' I put my arms around him. He cried into my neck. His tears dripped down my neck and into the depressions made by my collar bone, where they collected in two lakes, salt and clear.

After a trip to the garage to get the front banged out we were back on the road.

'I just don't know why they didn't do me for drunk driving,' he said. 'They didn't even give me the breathalyser, and me with the bottle of rum open under the seat.' He shook his head and looked out the window, away from the road. 'They must be pretty slow down here,' he concluded.

'I told them a moose ran in front of us and that you hadn't had a drink since the Maine border where you tried the rum and spat it out because it was too strong.'

He lit another cigarette. He looked at me in the rear-view mirror, eyebrows raised.

'How are you so sure they have moose in New York?'

SIXTEEN

B Y then I knew the entire repertoire of the Eagles; John
Denver and Glen Campbell songs had melded and fused
together and we'd heard the same Neil Young and Joni
Mitchell songs five hundred times.

'Gotta get an eight-track player.' He flicked the radio off as
they played 'Four Strong Winds' yet again.

On the outskirts of Cleveland before dusk hulking structures,
huge flat buildings and strange steel cranes lined the roadway.
Finally we arrived at a tall wood frame house.

'We're home.' He climbed stiffly out of the car.

'Well, well, you're Morag,' said a tall man with white hair.

Why were adults always stating the obvious?

'She's tired after the drive.' My grandfather shook his hand
and then turned to me. 'This is my father.'

'I thought you didn't have a father.' I peered at the man.

'Well,' Grandpa said, 'I do, and here he is, and you be nice to
him, 'cause I'm going to bed.'

He went inside and slept for twelve hours. I sat downstairs
with his father and his wife. My great-grandfather was a tall
man, about sixty-eight or so, who stooped on account of his
height. He had the same hawkish nose and frozen glass blue eyes
as my grandfather.

'Well,' he said (he began everything with 'well'), 'you must
be in school.' I shook my head, because my mouth was full of
the peanut-butter sandwich they had given me.

'No, I'm not because we're going to Mexico.'

They looked at one another, and then back at me.

'Mexico?'

I nodded.

'We thought you were coming here for a quick visit,' his wife said.

They looked at one another again.

'Does Christine – does your grandmother – know where you are?' he asked.

I shrugged my shoulders.

They telephoned Maryanne and Jessie. My great-grandfather spoke hurriedly and softly, all the while making his body a barrier between me and the voice coming out of the receiver, his hand cupped over the mouthpiece.

In the morning he came downstairs in his boxer shorts and undershirt. His hair stood straight up from his head.

'We spoke to Maryanne and Jessie,' my great-grandfather's wife said.

My grandfather glared at me.

'I didn't say nothing,' I protested.

'Anything,' he corrected.

'Sandy, she's had some sort of nervous collapse, you know.'

My grandfather sat down and ran his hand through his hair.

'John and I discussed it last night.' The woman looked over at her husband, who wouldn't look directly at my grandfather but kept his hands folded in his lap like a child. 'And we've decided that we're not letting you stay here. You have a duty to the child and to your wife to go back. You can leave this afternoon or not, but you're not staying under my roof while your wife suffers.'

'Okay. Fine,' my grandfather mumbled. 'We'll go back.' He got up and shuffled back upstairs.

'He'll start drinking.'

'No he won't,' my great-grandfather's wife retorted. 'When we put you in the room last night we got the rum bottle and

John took the keys and got the other four from the car.'

'He won't leave without them,' I said glumly.

'Well, we'll give them back. Anyway, he wouldn't be so stupid as to drink on the road.'

That afternoon, just after four, we were back on the road. 'Hit the road, Jack, and don't you come back no more no more ...' he sang. This time, I sat beside him, in the front seat.

The next day we saw the flashing signs. They said: FORT ERIE/CANADA.

'Are we going home, Grandpa?'

'We're going to Canada, yes.'

'I mean, are we going home?'

'I think I could use something to eat,' he said, quickly pulling off the highway and diving into a gas station.

Dust danced in the shafts of light. It was a thick light, golden and syrupy with the horizontal rays of a winter sun.

'You were always my darlin'. I'll never love anyone the way I loved you.'

'Please, Grandpa ...'

'You don't believe me but you have no idea. I've got no one to love me.' He raised his head from his hands. His palms and cheeks were wet.

'You're the only one in this world who loves me,' he sobbed.

I looked at him, his shoulders heaving, and I began to feel what women are taught to feel for such men; men who cry, men who profess their love, men whose very emotionalism strikes the wrong pitch on the wrong frequency on the wrong scale. I began to feel contempt.

We did not turn east as he had promised his father he would do, but headed west. Then we drove north, at first. Each town we passed had a Main Street, a Texaco station and a Woolworth's store. We drove underneath a low, hungry, grey sky, criss-crossed by electrical wires and tall, monolithic pylons stalking across the flatlands. Sound barriers shielded on either side of the highway, behind which lurked neat square row-houses with suburban back yards in which children played upon swing sets.

Dirty snow caked on the gas station signs, and men wearing down-filled coats, baseball caps and work boots shuffled desultorily along sidewalks. People spoke slowly.

'Where's the chocolate bars?' I asked storekeepers.

'Ahhh, Dunnnnnoooo,' they drawled, the words lasting so long I had already discovered the chocolate rack.

On the horizon I saw four strange hulking shapes standing tall against the sky. 'What are those things?' They looked like inverted tumblers.

'Nuclear reactors.' He cocked a suspicious eyebrow at them. 'That's the reason why they're all so slow around here.'

Bridget sent me dresses made from cloth patterned with stars, giraffes and swimming fishes. The dresses were supposed to wrap around the body, to cling to the sharp bones and thin hips of a child. I saw black women with drooping breasts wear them in *National Geographic*, the only other magazine in our house besides *Reader's Digest*.

'You dress weird,' is what they said at school, when I made the mistake of wearing one once.

The dresses hung at the back of my closet like carcasses in an abattoir, covered in plastic, waiting for the return of my body and for the sun that never came.

'Do you want me to drive?' I joked.

He could hardly keep his eyes on the road.

'I'll stop.' We screeched to a halt alongside the cement docks.

We were in Sault Ste Marie, and giant cranes stood rusting in the sunlight, poised on the edge of the lake like they were about to fall in. He got out of the car and without a word started walking off in the direction of a few dilapidated wooden warehouses. I climbed on the hood of the car, which was still warm. I was sitting there when he returned half an hour later, squinting into the afternoon sun.

'I used to work here, you know,' he said.

I swivelled my head around.

'There's nothing here,' I said. A few seagulls circled aimlessly, otherwise there wasn't a soul or a ship in sight.

'Would you believe that these docks were once chock full with ships waiting to be loaded and unloaded?'

'No.'

'Let's go.' He climbed quickly into the car.

It is 1933. He stands in front of the cranes on the container pier, their rust bones creaking into the sky behind him where the smokestack of a barge spews soot. There are four of them lined up. Two of them in grease-stained workshirts and denims flank the others, who stand in shirts, ties and suspenders, and clutching suit jackets. The one on the left, the tall one, is good-looking, almost like a movie star. He has a languid, sweet smile. My grandfather is the shortest. The sleeves of his greasy workshirt are rolled up well above his elbows. His forearms are long and thick. The hand, which rests on his thigh, clutches a cigarette. He is thick-barrelled, sturdy, short-legged. He has the cocky posture of a young gorilla, and a dangerous smile, a smile that seems intoxicated with the newfound possibilities of male conquest and of self-hatred.

He looks like a young boy from the sticks, which is what he is. A young man from nowhere, selling his body to shovel coal into the furnaces of the lake barge boats. This is how he fed his mother and his sisters during the Depression. His face is young – he must be about eighteen or nineteen – and fat. He looks like the rooster before a cockfight; he looks like a prize boxer.

He looks angry.

In 1945, he holds the dog up by its front paws, laying its white belly bare to the camera. He is twenty-five but looks thirty-five. His face has shrunk to half its width in the photograph taken on the large barge docks. He has a small square moustache. It's this and his mean eyes that make him look like Hitler. But there is something else: he's just come out of a burn ward. He has very little left of his eyebrows and eyelashes. The texture of his skin is different, like moist bread compared to lightly done toast. He looks like a matinée villain: small, well-sprung, thin-faced, a chilling, vampire gaze. As if he is sizing you up to see how much blood you have in you; how much he can extract. He doesn't smile. He looks rather suave. The way murderers look when they are trying to attract potential victims.

'This is the breadbasket of the world,' he announced. I knew where he had got this from. The sign when we crossed the border said: SASKATCHEWAN: THE BREADBASKET OF CANADA.

'I thought that was the Ukraine,' I said.

'Never you mind. That's a communist place,' he growled and switched the radio station.

The meridians passed in a steady procession. Miles of long golden stocks of winter wheat fluttered in the breeze, a thousand heads of gold-red hair. Now and then the horizon was pierced by a grain elevator or a farmhouse, painfully white against the bucking piebald mustang sky.

The country was like a film reel, endlessly unwinding itself in front of us as we advanced towards the Pacific. There were countless frames of white fields punctured by pockets of desert-yellow wheat, a sky always blue, looking strangely like the dishes in cheap Chinese restaurants where we sometimes stopped to eat. 'This is how man was meant to be,' he said. 'On the move. You don't stop for very long or you get caught.'

The meridians passed underneath us with their metronome precision, counting in the 4/4 clackety-clack time of folksongs and freight-trains.

He was mad again. The storm had come over the fields of his mind and now it sat, broiling just above his right eye.

'Who are you, Morag?'

'You know who I am.'

'Who do you think you are?' He said, and it sounded like a threat.

'I'm me.'

'And who's that?' he asked. 'Do you know how lucky you are that your grandmother and I took you in?' He leaned towards me, advancing on my face like a brush fire. He took me by the shoulders, shook me.

'You owe your goddamn life to us, and don't forget it.'

I tried to get away. He shook me harder. I thought my brains were going to spill out onto the carpet.

Finally he let me go, shoving me over toward the wall. I sank down with the small of my back against its coolness, clutching my knees. The consommé brown of the hotel room, the washed-out wallpaper, the beef-coloured bedspread, all began to swim before me.

'I'm going out,' he said.

'Don't leave me here,' I wailed.

'I'll leave you wherever I goddamn want to.'

He was on his power trip now. I heard him turn the key in the latch, locking me in. I started to panic, but stifled it. I heard the car pull out of the driveway, the squeal of the tyres as he burned rubber on the asphalt. And then nothing, until the morning.

'What the hell are you doing down there?' he asked, towering above me.

'I fell asleep,' I said from the floor. It was morning.

'Well, get up and let's get some breakfast. I'm starving.' He put his hand on my head. 'How about pancakes? Your favourite.' He smacked his lips and we headed over to the motel dining room.

SEVENTEEN

B Y the time we reached the Rockies it was starting to look like spring. I was allowed to stick my head out of the window and drink in the slipstream as we sailed into the western sun. We had established a rhythm. In truck stops, motel diners, and gas station restaurants we ordered the same things and said little to each other as we perused the menu or read the placemats. I sometimes kept the placemats for my scrapbook of our trip – *Cree Chiefs since 1700* showed all the chiefs in their incredible headdresses. *Fruehauf Trucks: the workhorse engine* depicted the evolution of Fruehauf cabs since the 1930s. *Montana: the plateau state* showed Devils' Peak bleeding out from around our melmac plates of scrambled eggs and bacon. Near Drumheller, the *Badlands* placemat was ringed by dinosaurs whose skeletons had been found around there: Tyrannosaurus Rex, Stegosaurus, Pteranodon.

We watched the ceramic sun set on the rim of the southwest as we drove through the desert badlands of southern Alberta and northern Montana. In Jasper a mountain goat came right up to the car and stuck his head, horns and all, inside and licked my nose. Through Kicking Horse Pass, through the lush, fruit-stocked valley, the Okanagan winter was breaking up; the spring was warm and thick. We opened our windows and stuck our arms out. Each week on the road had brought a new sign of life: ice breaking up on a lake, the sound of birds again, slush piled on the underside of car bumpers. I tried to imagine this land in summer. Now it looked as though it was just recovering from some unknown devastation, the trees ripped bare, the lunar landscape of the wheatfields slapped down by the snow and frost. But here in this fruit-stocked valley the trees were laced with small green buds, and the ice on the roadside melted of its own accord by ten in the morning.

I was amazed, zipping by this euphoric renewal in our slush-encrusted Chevette. No country transforms itself from winter to summer as suddenly and as beautifully as ours does.

We sailed into Chiliwack, BC. We would stay with Aunt Helen a few days, and then go on to Vancouver where Grandpa's other sister lived. The town was much the same as the endless Ohio towns we had passed by; but at the end of the main street was this stupendous mountain, symmetrically cutting the town in half and thrusting up into the clouds.

Helen opened the door.

'Oh and this must be Morag,' she said. 'And haven't you grown. I wouldn't have recognized you . . .' she cooed. 'She'll be a woman in no time.' She took my grandfather's coat and scarf.

'What's a woman, Grandpa?' I asked, struggling to get my scarf off without choking myself.

'Never you mind.' He gave me a baleful look. 'You don't have to worry about that for some time yet.'

'Could you take your shoes off, you two,' Aunt Helen asked a little too pleasantly, a note of irritation in her voice. 'I just put in new wall-to-wall shag carpeting. What do you think of it, Sandy?'

'Very nice,' he called as we struggled with our shoes. He leaned over in my direction and grumbled. 'Looks like a goddamn dead animal's been stretched out on the floor.'

Later, after we had eaten, she looked at my grandfather hard. 'Sandy,' she sighed. 'You've got to go back.'

He put his cup down on the saucer with a clatter.

'I can get work out here.'

'For Jesus' sake, think of Morag.'

'We'll be on our way then, Helen, thanks.'

'I'm calling the police,' she said.

He got up, fetched his cap and his car keys, and we were on our way to Vancouver. On the outskirts of town he stopped the car and went into a payphone box.

'Who're you calling?'

'None of your business.'

'Are you calling Grandma?'

'I said it's none of your business,' he yelled from inside the booth.

I hung my head out the window.

'You don't have to shout.'

'I'M NOT SHOUTING,' he shouted.

At some point in British Columbia I saw seagulls hundreds of miles inland, and thought of the *Tigh Mhór*, our dog and her, all alone in the evenings with her solitaire deck and my grandfather's diabolical mother for company. I realized, suddenly, that I hadn't thought of her for weeks.

When he had made his call we drove on through the small towns of southern British Columbia.

'I made a deal with God,' he said to me as we drove out of another highwayside motel.

'What?'

'I told God that if I could have you all to myself then I would take the consequences.'

He's drunk, I thought. But where'd he stash the rum?

'You don't understand, do you?'

'No,' I humphed, and concentrated on the blurred landscape outside the window.

'You're my whole life, that's what I'm Jesus trying to tell you. My life's over. And I'm nothing. I ain't never been anything I wanted to be and it's over for me. I don't want to lose you. I'm afraid I'll lose myself.'

'Do you lose people like you lose a pair of mittens?'

'You lose people because they stop loving you and start loving someone else.'

'I thought you loved someone forever.'

'No, that's a myth.'

'What's a myth?'

'A fancy story. Don't they teach you anything in school?'

'I'd be in school now if you hadn't taken me away.'

He looked troubled.

'We'll have to get you back,' he said.

'I thought we were going to Mexico.'

'Another time.'

'What about Australia?' I wailed.

'We'll get there some other time.'

He sold the Chevette in Vancouver and we flew all the way home.

The picture book of World History that Bridget had sent me showed that Bucephalus was a Thessalian stallion, black and big. In the picture, his eyes rolled back in his head in the same way Philip of Macedon must have seen young boys' eyes roll backward in sexual ecstasy. The stallion's muscles were living things, huge great sinuous snakes beneath his coat, which shone like a thousand battle-won tomorrows. It was obvious to everyone who saw him, that the horse was one of those rare creatures, built to absorb all space and all possible meaning. The stallion reared and bucked, lashing out with his hind legs, unleashing from them a preternatural force of torque and spew.

Alexander's trick is now famous. He saw that it was the horse's fear of his own shadow fluttering in front of him that had made him jump so. So he simply turned the horse's head into the sun, where there was no shadow for him to see. The stallion calmed down immediately, dazzled by the light and the disappearance of the phantom animal that had been creeping over the ground in front of him.

Bucephalus was not mean. He was afraid. But his fear expressed itself as cruelty.

Strange that a boy only eight years old should have been the one to recognize his fear, and then blind him to it.

SPRING

EIGHTEEN

WHEN we got back, Grandma looked like a pale reflection of herself. Her hair had gone white overnight, it seemed. Her face was thin, as if two fish lines had been cast on either side of her mouth and were hauling it down. Her lips were sour.

In my room, the old warped curves of the wall were foreign now. The sound of the bare branches of the apple tree swatting my window sounded like the tune of isolation. She wouldn't look at me. Whenever I caught a good view of her face there were tears in her eyes. I felt like a murderer. He felt the same, judging from his slouching dog's posture as he skulked around the house.

When I went back to school in early April I was something of a minor hero. I had been across the country, I had been kidnapped. There had been RCMP cruisers on alert all across the country, looking for our licence plate.

'What's the Rockies like?'

'You see cowboys out West?'

I had come back full of my own questions.

'Grandma, what's a mother?'

'Never you mind.'

'What's a father?'

'Don't bother yourself with that. You're mine and that's all you need to know.'

'The kids at school say I don't belong to you,' I pressed on.

'They say I'm supposed to have a mother and a father but I don't.'

'Well that's a lot of malarkey. You listen to what your grandmother says. I know the truth, and I'm telling it to you. It's as true as I'm standing here. So you ignore that baloney they talk. All right?'

It was true that never once in her life did she lie to me.

Something called a Social Worker came to the Big House. The country had sent her to investigate the 'kidnapping'. The woman took me off to my own room and asked me to take my shirt off.

'Why?' I said.

'I just want to have a look to make sure you're all right.'

'You mean you want to see if they've been hitting me?'

'You're smart for your age,' she said coolly.

'Nobody hits me,' I said. 'I can take care of myself.'

'I'm sure you can,' she said smoothly. 'But if you take off your shirt I'll give you a lollipop.'

Downstairs my grandmother smoked desperately. She squirmed in her seat when we reappeared and the Social Worker began to ask her questions.

He opened the door and propped up his fishing rod. He had been casting off the jetty for cod and hadn't seen the car come.

'Who're you?' He was already angry.

'Are you Alexander Neil MacAulay?' the woman asked, her voice official.

'No, I'm the goddamn Pope,' Grandpa snapped.

'I'm Ms X from Social Services.'

'I know who you fucking are. Who gave you permission to enter my house? Have you got a warrant to enter?'

'I can come with a policeman who will have a warrant, if that's what you want,' she said.

'Look, I don't want no trouble,' he said, sighing heavily. The fight just left him, all of a sudden. 'I don't like other people poking their noses into my business. Now, have you had a cup of tea?' He put the kettle on, and sat down.

Half an hour later they were all chatting amiably.

'Oh yes, I knew your father. We worked at the base together. Fifty-five, I think it was. How's Malcolm?'

'Well, he's getting on.' The woman sipped her tea. 'His back isn't so good anymore.'

Later, when they had banished me from the kitchen, I listened above the register.

'I can appreciate what you're trying to do, Sandy,' the woman said. 'It can't be easy bringing up a child at your age . . .'

'Well, I'm not ready for the grave yet.'

'But all the same, you can't go taking her off across the country.'

'I don't think you're the one to tell me what I can and can't do.'

'Don't you care that your wife had to be hospitalized with worry?'

He was silent for a while. He looked at the young woman, his hands turned open on his knees like explanations.

'I'm not a monster, you know,' he said, softly.

'Where's she gone?' I asked him, even though I could see he was in a surly mood.

'To town.'

'Great-Grandma's gone shopping?' I couldn't think of another reason why anyone would go to Town.

'She's moved out,' he said sullenly. 'She's bought herself one of them retirement condominiums in Glace Bay.'

'Morag,' hissed my grandmother, who suddenly appeared around the corner. 'Come away from your grandfather. Your great-grandmother's sold the house out from underneath us,' she explained. I had a vision of the house being whisked out from under us like magicians pull tablecloths from underneath fine china and cutlery. But then, the cutlery is left in place. From that night on, we were out on the street.

It had to be brought along the highway by a huge contraption, a flatbed trunk which took up more than half the road so that oncoming cars had to duck off onto the shoulder to get by. When they had taken off all the ropes and straps and had fired up the crane machine on the back of the truck, they picked up the trailer like a cat would pick up its kitten by the scruff of the neck, and plunked it down on a piece of land my grandfather had cleared.

A couple of weeks later we moved into the trailer. Our new home was a pale, faded-mustard yellow, with fibreglass siding. Long and narrow, it rested many feet above the ground. The door was as high as my grandmother's head.

'We won't be able to even get into that thing until your grandfather builds a porch,' Grandma said.

That thing, she had called it.

My grandfather built a porch in three days solid. It was long – long enough to put out a couple of lawn chairs for sitting on, long enough to skin a deer on, and it had steps leading precipitously down to the ground. The Americans to whom the Big House had been sold were coming to take it over in a few months' time. So we piled our belongings in the back of a pickup truck and drove slowly up the hill, a couple of hundred yards along the highway, and we turned into our new driveway.

'I've invited Dan over for some tea,' he told her. 'We're building a smokehouse this afternoon and setting up some nets tomorrow. And Miriam's coming too, this afternoon. She's stopping by on her way up to Jessie and Maryanne's.'

Miriam lived far away, up near Cape North, and she was French. Not French-French; her family must have been ten generations removed from France, but she spoke only French and Gaelic. She had a little English, but it wasn't very good.

When she visited she would speak Gaelic to them and French to me.

'The child has to learn the language,' Miriam was saying to my grandparents in Gaelic. She stood there in the new kitchen, heavy in her floral dress and bookish in her tightly bound dark hair and thick-rimmed spectacles. She had been a schoolteacher, and she still dressed like one. She took me outside, down into the fields below. Tree trunks littered the hill. A black acrid smoke still hung in the air, from where he had burnt the young alders and other scrub bushes that morning.

'*Eh regarde ton petit univers.*' She pointed to the various features of the landscape. '*Les collines, la montagne, la mer, les gîts, les pêches, le chemin, le pont, si grand et magnifique . . .*' She pointed down to the hulking A-frame of Seal Island bridge, just visible from our new land.

We stood there awhile, talking, and then turned to go back.

'*Enfin, t'aimes la roulotte, ta nouvelle maison?*'

'*Non,*' I replied, trying to think why not. '*C'est trop petite.*'

'*Tu sais, ton arrière-grand'mère est une vraie salope,*' she said. *You know, your great-grandmother is a real bitch.*

I smiled up at her, nodding, and we waved to my grandmother, who watched us from the kitchen window.

Inside the trailer everything was new. New sink, new fridge, new carpet. It smelled unlike anything I had smelled before. There was no familiar must, the kind that old furniture seemed to breed on its own, no smell of old wood, no cracked but heroic linoleum that had lain on the same floor for fifty years. Everything was left behind in the Big House. There was simply no room in the trailer for the mahogany chest, the stacks of china dishes it contained, the enormous round dining table, not to mention the commodes, dressers, and bureaux, shelves and trunks. The trailer came furnished with plywood doors, Formica tables and vinyl chairs.

Worse, our new fridge was lime green, instead of white, so

we couldn't project onto that. There wasn't a white surface in sight. The fortnightly slide shows stopped. My grandmother and I took to holding up the slides to the strong kitchen light and squinting through their transparent covers.

'I think that's Bridget,' she scowled. 'The one on the far right.'

'How can you tell?' I asked her, screwing up my eyes.

'The rest of them are black.'

'What's that?'

'What do you mean, what's that?' She took the slide down from the light and scowled at me. 'Black is the darkies,' she said.

'What's a darkie?'

'People with dark skin. They come from Africa.'

'Are there any darkies here?'

She thought for a minute. 'There's the Robertsons,' she said, referring to a family who lived on the South Side.

'But they're from Sierra Leone.' She put a slide back neatly in the box. 'Wherever that is.'

Bridget kept sending the slides, packed in their neat plastic Kodak boxes developed in and labelled in somewhere called Harare. But it wasn't the same. We needed the projector to blow up their proportions, to make them real.

The *Tigh Mhór* sat empty on the other side of the hayfield. In the evenings that spring I went down the driveway and leant on the old post at the edge of the field. I picked tall sweetgrass and sucked on the ends. It felt familiar down there, comfortable. Except the house was locked and no one was at home. Up in the trailer we could barely pass each other in the narrow corridor. There were no more stairs to run down in the morning, and no garden, which rapidly became overgrown. With spring came the strawberries sending out the thin capillaries of their runners to weave a redrushing quilt across the ground, impatient to bear the red blood corpuscles of fruit.

From my perch, a half-mile and a field away from the trailer,

I could hear their voices. They were flung out of turmoil. It was becoming twilight, the hour of the Trickster. If I did not leave the Big House soon I would meet him or her in the long driveway. At twilight by the shore I would see strange forms in the woods. Great, hairy lurking men would leap across falling trees and appear for a moment on a clay-coloured promontory by the sea. Only the dog and I would see him. I suppose it must have been a bear, but its eyes were red-ringed and wild.

The shouting came louder.

Bitch. Drunk. Responsibility.

The cricket's voluble speech rose and fell along the banks of the highway, forward and back like waves. The warm evening stillness and the gravel dust from the shoulder of the road burned in my throat.

The voices crescendoed.

At the trailer, conversations were being lost or won.

NINETEEN

W E ran across the highway and scrambled up the embankment on the other side, and then up along the old
overgrown track through the black woods. Grandma
tripped on a tree root. Then I went down. We pulled one
another up in turn, although I could do little but tug on her arm
insistently.

'Get up, Grandma, get up.'

That was the first night we ran across the highway, hunched
low like thieves, avoiding the yellow sweep of the tall highway
light. Then we were in the ditch, clumping through stagnant
water and mud. We crashed through the lower branches of tall
pines until we reached the cabin.

Inside it was pitch dark. Before we had a chance to light the
kerosene lamps we heard a strange rustling, like the whispers of
people turning over in their beds at night. Then there was a
sudden rushing about our heads. Little balls of air brushed our
hair and our faces.

'Jesus Mary and Joseph!' my grandmother screamed. 'It's bats.'
She covered her head with her hands and ran out the door. I
saw a white plastic washtub on the dresser, and picked it up with
both hands and raised it above my head. I wielded its hollow
side at the phantom airborne creatures. When I felt the wings
beat against the side of the tub I dipped it down and shooed
them out.

'I hate bats,' she said, her mouth set in a thin determined line, which meant that she'd got over her fright and felt silly.

There was one bed, made of boards and a straw mattress and an old damp blanket. The place smelled of kerosene and camphor and mildew. She got into the bed fully clothed and pulled me in beside her. I wanted to keep the lamp on. But she wouldn't let me. He might see the light, after all.

'Are you warm enough?' she asked from beside me in the cabin bed.

'I'm all right.' I was freezing. It was early spring but the frost still clipped the night air, and the damp in the cabin was permanent.

She reached out and dimmed the kerosene lamp. We could see our reflections in the top of the arabesqued glass flame cover. Two people, our faces huge and our small bodies stretching behind us like a desert landscape.

The next morning we went back down the hill, and crossed the highway to the trailer. The car was parked at a crazy angle in the driveway. The dog greeted us, frenzied with joy at seeing rational people. He sat in the kitchen on one of the cheap chrome chairs. He was playing the fiddle, a tune I knew well.

'*Mo' Mhithair*' A haunting tune, desperate in its sadness. It's like a slide guitar weeping down the chord progression from G to A to D, sliding down into remorse and regret and wallowing there in a manner which is quite voluptuous. To the ear it is either sopping with the usual lumpen sentiment men seem to reserve for their first lovers, or it is a sleek, fleshless lament for the end of unconditional love.

In English, its name is 'My Mother'.

The cod stocks were thick that spring. They swam in their millions off the concrete jetty. We had only to put our hands in and scoop them out, one by one. The came willingly, putting up only a small fight before their gills stopped quivering for water. We cut them open and put great chunks of salt on their flesh, which was seared white by the contact. And they bled. I was surprised to see that fish had blood. I thought water flowed through their veins. We smoked some in the smokehouse in the twilight of the spring evening. They went in white and came out a fluorescent yellow, like the eyes of goats.

I lay in the silence those nights, rigid with listening. It had become an obsession to hear through the silence, not to be confounded by the prospect of hearing nothing except the crows' metal cries of woe and the crickets chirring. Before sleep I liked to chart the way my mind fractured into fragments of images: of German soldiers goosestepping, of vultures perching on top of rusting Victorian railway carriages and of a woman whose hair is woven into thick braids and who is standing on a jetty thrust out into a wide-hipped river.

The nets were strung high up between two sturdy birch trees, and they swayed in the wind with their cargo of cod. The evenings turned amber, the sun advanced on a bank of clouds from the west, and our arm of gold, our *bras d'or*, stretched languidly out into the night and went to sleep beside the sea. From my room at the back I heard the nets – their groaning, imploring, the whisperings between the birch-tree reticences – I heard their message as they swung from north to south in the night wind. They said: *Africa*.

She was drunk.

'You're the only one who he'll listen to. You're the only one who makes any sense to him. You merely came on the scene at the right time. All you had to do was exist.'

She became very irritable when she drank.

She was rocking back and forth in her rocking chair, talking to herself. I ran to my room.

'That's right,' she called behind me. 'You can run but you can't hide.'

There's a scene with him, too, in the very same kitchen, at night. I get up often at about two or three in the morning and sit there with him or her, whichever is up at the time. With him, I usually play cards: a game of crib or poker. Tonight, though, he just sits there.

'She wouldn't touch me after that.' His hands flutter in anger. He looks at me across the table as if I were another adult, another man, even, someone his own age.

'She wanted a child,' he continues. 'Well, she got what she wanted, and then she wouldn't have anything more to do with me.'

His voice cracks on the last word. He is so forlorn in that moment, he looks so abandoned, that he could very well be a child and not a man whose age I do not know because I cannot conceive of being that old.

'Well,' he says, 'isn't it time you were getting back to bed? You've got school in the morning.'

My grandfather and I are waltzing together. I am standing on his toes. I have my arms around his waist and my head pushed hard into his stomach. He smells of Old Spice aftershave. He smells dry. He hardly ever sweats – he is that fit. We are waltzing to a Joe Cormier tune. My grandmother comes into the living room from the bedroom. Grandma looks like a cross between Bette Davis and Joan Crawford, her beauty slightly retrograde, slightly exhausted. She comes, walking quickly, but slows down when she sees us dancing. She stands on the threshold of the door, a thin bird of a smile fluttering on her face. But her eyes remain hurt and as distant from the smile as the southern Florida estuaries to where the local birds migrate in the winter. I see her every time we twirl around. I catch her face and then she is gone, obscured by the whirlwind that is taking me around and around, waltzing in the private ballroom of love that he has constructed just for me.

Thick heat, like something you can touch, hold in your hand. Warm gelatin hardening in a bowl. Steam trapped in a balloon.

Earth smells, even the green of the leaves is a tangible smell, those leaves that go on forever into the sky. Red earth, like ochre. A wind that comes off a continent, the bottom end, where it is narrowing, where the gap between the oceans has been tapered down into a field across which drift electrical storms and vast, hulking clouds, the reflection of whole cities travelling overhead.

Snakes in the grass at night. Their oblong eyes, sweet and vicious, mesmerizing their prey. Killed with a shovel by the village man protecting his hut. Mashed into a bloody pulp, their skin remaining intact. Like you would skin a mackerel, then leaving the black rough casing in limp rolls by the cutting board.

'I love you to death,' he said. 'You're all I live for. I'd die without you.'

Who is this person who is not living for themself?

Why are they living for me? What is so remarkable about me?

He hit me. The blow came down on my head, a thick helmet made of iron, and sat there. I felt the storm of annihilation sweeping through me, its shock waves flattening my ears back against my head like a mad horse. Then I felt relaxed, all the tension drained out of me, water out of the holes in a sieve.

He said: 'I love you more than life itself.'

'If you ever so much as touch me again,' I said, 'I'll kill you.'

He looked at me and his eyes were so sad I wanted to shoot him, just to put him out of his misery. Like a sick dog, or a horse with a broken leg. I thought: Who am I to threaten to kill a broken man?

In early May icebergs began to appear off the east coast of the island. My grandfather and I drove out to Louisbourg to see them; he loved to watch their mountain bulk drifting by on the calm water. Some were enormous, their peaks rising to staggering heights, hundreds of feet in the air.

They drifted by in the distance, five or ten miles out to sea, melting with each spring-warm wave lapping against their flanks. We had brought our binoculars with us and we could see every detail; their fittings and riggings. I thought they looked like the apparition of an ocean liner, a pale stately ghost of the *Titanic*, which had sunk not very far away. Once they reached the southernmost part of the island they were nearly melted.

The sun rose higher and the morning turned sere and white; the milky sky, the gypsum cliffs, the mottled pink of the cockles' shells, all began to throb and whiten like hot phosphorus.

The morning wind picked up, and the sea woke up, spread out its billowing ermine silks, and set to rocking. We turned back to the icebergs, our binoculars in synchronicity as we surveyed the mint blues of their crevices and the dead purples of their peaks. As the sunlight hit them a thousand half-pastels sprang from their previously monotone white flanks.

'They're mostly underneath the water, you know. It's just a smidgin of them that you can see. There's twice or three times as much bulk underneath the water. That's what the *Titanic* hit: the underwater part.'

Just then one of the smaller icebergs pitched and yawed slightly, and plopped over on its side. Out of the water came a tremendous ridge of blue ice, taller than the floating peak that had tipped over.

'See?' he pointed. 'Just like your grandmother.'

'What?'

He took the binoculars away and let them dangle against his chest, suspended by their straps. In the distance the iceberg wobbled uncertainly.

He looked down at me.

'Mostly beneath the surface.'

When his fists met her flesh, or any flesh, I could see the rapture spreading underneath his mask of concentrated anger. He did not despise her. He loved her. Roseate spots of wonderment stained his cheek. I have never heard such a loving sound as that of the impact of his flesh upon her flesh. It was a loving gesture; *yes*, he thought; *I love her now.* It was his structure, that of the lover and of the hitter, and hers was bound up in that too.

If someone's structure, no matter how mauled, is taken away from them they only cry and cry like a baby. Like when the lover leaves – suddenly you are without lineaments, without form, and therefore void; the props holding up the circus tent collapse. The trapeze hangs limp as an unmoved cock, buffeted by the wind. The animals all die from thirst in their cages. Sequins fade to fish-scale translucence.

She had never been brought up to take the contorted shapes she later had to assume. She had been brought up straight and true, in the neat angles of a hexagon. Six brothers and sisters; hay-rides in the summer, maple syrup gathering in March. They had lived in the Garden of Eden. Why should anything bad ever happen to her?

She was an orange and he stuck cloves into her: juicy flesh seared by spice. All that innocent, wet love burnt by a substance whose mercurial flash and bitter taste was like quicklime, or lye. Her hands touched his anger and they burned dry and cracked.

She was the ascendant; she was going up and up. She knew this because she was named after Christ. She lifted her minor cross, and trudged up the hills of years. In the end she was the one who rose. She took the wolves of his anger with her; I saw their red and yellow eyes blinking in the serene night, disguised as the celestial jewels of the planets. She set them free as they howled for dawn. He heard them, and he mourned their silver, freakish faces and the company they had given him over the years.

This man, with whom her life bound up, almost accidentally, this man from up the road. She might never have left the farmhouse to walk into that thirty years' worth of structure she came to inhabit, her structure as the object that received the blows of his love. So that she would be better off today if she

134

were still there, haunting the empty rooms of her childhood house, looking for the ghosts of her brothers and sisters, sitting on the metal skeletons of the old beds, gazing out the window and watching the moon rising in her eyes.

I can see her there: it is midnight in the abandoned Garden of Eden. A woman sits in the empty room; she is the only witness left to testify to the gifts given to her by her life, to the beauty of the story, to the quotidian inconsequentialities stretching before her, her years with him.

'He's sick,' she told me. 'He's got cancer. They gave him pills and told him he couldn't drink while he was on medication, but he drinks anyway.'

He seemed to be getting more and more unbalanced; coming home later, in worse and worse shape. I feared the nights now more than I ever had – they were the unformed time, the time of chaos and of white headlights scything a path through the night.

I looked at her, and she at me.

'He's going to kill himself,' she said.

The bear-prints and the mountain-lion tracks were visible only in snow or clay, or in mud that had frozen with an overnight frost. He taught me to distinguish between them, and other prints too. We would put our hands in them, lay them out inside the print. We would look at the digits, their configuration, the shape of the claws, whether the animal had stood square, like bears, or with one hind foot thrown back and out, like cougars and lynxes.

The gun rack was positioned directly above the head of the bed, in between Grandpa's and Grandma's pillows. Five guns lay one on top of the other. On the bottom was the .410, a small shotgun, next was the .22, a good small-animal hunting rifle. Next up lay the 3006, and the .303, the big moose and deer guns, and then the 12 gauge, a reasonably powerful shotgun that he did not really like to use because of the mess it created.

He was teaching me to shoot already, even though it was illegal, even though it was dangerous. He trusted me; he had confidence in me. I was working my way up the gun rack from the small guns on the bottom rungs. By the time I left my grandfather's house I was more than proficient in loading and firing the .22.

With the crack of the hair trigger came the flying of snow in all directions. On the lake the loons squawked at the sound, losing their elegant voices, and soaked one another with the water sprayed off their wings during their quick ascent. The dozing squirrels woke and the bears swivelled their amber eyes.

'All this chaos is the achievement of man,' my grandfather told me.

Otherwise the world consists of only the powdered snow-dust as it flies from the trees, the icicles as they drop precipitously from eaves, the water leaping from the lake under the bodies of the ascending loons, the fear in the thick eyes of the bear, the grace in the deer as she vaults a log, and the shattered silence of sky and of earth, of water and of fire.

A warm spring day, and were out walking through the woods from the Big House to the shore.

'Look,' I pointed to the mushrooms growing bulbous under the tree. 'There's the old woman's kidneys.'

'That's right,' he nodded. He stopped in front of the tree and bent down so that his hunting jacket was level with me, peering at them.

Dan had told us a story, one that explained the origins of the fungus. All mushrooms had come from the kidneys of an old woman. When she died, her organs turned to fungus, and that was why they grew in the forest.

'Listen,' my grandfather said, straightening up. 'Dan told you that story to make sure you don't touch those, you hear? Not under any circumstances. Cause if you even lick your fingers,' and he pulled off one of his gloves and demonstrated, dragging the pad of his index finger across his tongue. 'Like that,' he finished, putting his hand back in his glove. 'If you even do that after touching one of them,' he pointed to them, 'they'll kill you. Those mushrooms were once a bad woman,' he said, repeating the story. 'She was all bitter and twisted, so her kidneys turned to fungus, and she came to lay right there.'

'What was the matter with her?' I asked.

He shrugged. 'She was poisonous.'

We walked on toward the shore, leaving the mushrooms behind, lurking plump and docile under the tree.

Bad woman. Woman losing her kidneys, woman turning to fungus. Woman going back to nature.

Woman disintegrating.

TWENTY

BECAUSE it was late May the storm caught us by surprise. It started with hail, followed by strange lightning that streaked across the sky like sheets of metal shaken out of God's hand. Then the temperature dropped by ten degrees, and the snow began.

He was already strange when he left. He had gone out without his snow tyres on, had taken them off the car that very weekend. We spent a tense evening playing cards at the kitchen table, watching the cars pass at steadily lengthening intervals on the highway as the weather worsened. Sometimes we could barely hear ourselves for the wind beating against the fibreglass siding. The dog quivered beneath the table.

At one point my grandmother got up abruptly and went down the dark corridor, into their bedroom. When she returned she was carrying the .22.

'Here,' she said, handing it to me. 'You load this. I don't know how.' She thumped a box of bullets on the table.

I looked at her.

'Go ahead,' she said. 'Do it.'

'These are the wrong calibre.' I eyed the box. 'They're for the .303.'

'Well, go get the right ones.'

I went down into the dark bedroom. I put the chair against their wardrobe and clambered up to the top, where he kept the ammunition. There were no .22 bullets. I remembered that he had the last box in the trunk of the car, left over from March when we had gone out shooting rabbits.

I returned to the kitchen carrying the .303.

'What's that?'

'There aren't any .22 bullets. So I took this one.'

'That's too big,' she said. 'I don't know how to shoot that one.'

'I do.'

'Go away with you. You're eight years old. You can't even lift that.'

I lifted it up and put it in the crook of my arm. I looked right down the barrel at her. I was a big girl for my age. It might knock me over, but I could still fire it and hit a more or less stationary target at a hundred yards.

'All right,' she said, convinced, grabbing the gun from me. 'What the Christ does he teach you out in those woods?'

'What do we need the gun for?'

She brushed a tendril of her hair from her face. 'I'm not sure,' she said, slowly, carefully. 'I want to take it with us. I think we might have to go to the cabin.' She looked out the window, nervous, as if he might appear just because she had said the words.

'Why?'

'Don't why me. Just load the gun.'

I took the big bullets, heavy in my fingers, and loaded it. I had never loaded the .303, so I did it just the same as the .22, missing the small slim bullets and the ease with which they slipped into the chamber.

The stove clock ticked. The wind against the side of the trailer made the kettle rattle on its electric burner. Every once in a while she would look at it as if were about to jump off the stove and come sailing right for us.

We could not see anything outside the windows, besides the night thrashing itself to bits.

The moment: even now I live in that moment only. A moment

drunk on its own voluptuousness, grotesquely expanded until it comes to mean more than what happened inside its lineaments. This is the hyperbolic, trumped-up universe of the *doer*. The rest of the time I am dead, for all purposes; dead as Alexander in his unknown tomb, as if my grandfather had left me there on the kitchen floor, dead and bleeding into the linoleum, my stupid eight years of age secreting its unknowingness, its futurelessness, into the linoleum's woodstove-and-butterfly pattern.

I come alive only to live in the shadow of myself; I am a ghost, slightly auto-cannibalistic, turned in on myself; I come alive only to feel again what I felt. And what I felt was this: *alive.*

It all happened very quickly. Afterwards she had telephoned her friend Rita and Rita had come and driven us out there. The tyres burned the asphalt as we peeled out of the driveway. Our breaths gouged deep in our chests, like the breaths of race runners.

Green light seeped out from the seams surrounding the speed-ometer and the clock on Rita's dashboard panel. Beneath the headlights flashed broken white lines of the highway meridians.

'God provides for those who do not sin,' said my grandmother.

I thought of the trailer, which He had provided for us. His voice echoed through my empty fluorescent night-mind: *We must have committed a few for him to give us this shitbox.*

In the years to come we never talked about what happened that night. It was part of the universal survivor's code: you dismiss the importance of talking about it, because what good could that possibly do? As with sex, for instance; which derives its power from its lack of language; there was this feeling that what is least spoken about is in fact most real.

Later that night, after the frozen, winged moment, she does not look behind her to see the dog standing in the screen doorway, nearly frantic. She does not turn into a pillar of salt. She knows her Bible stories and has no desire to become Lot's wife.

From this moment on, the dead years are either over or they have just begun.

ARDOUR

TWENTY-ONE

THE goat leaves Chile's aluminium desert at Antofagasta and skips across his broken line into the Pacific, passing just underneath the Tubuai islands of French Polynesia and across the Tonga ridge. He does not hit land of any significant size again until he meets the town where I live, which he streaks through without bothering to stop, rapt in his meridian's obsession with division, passing through the emerald mines of Queensland, the flat palm of the Gibson desert and straight through Lake Disappointment, neatly carving its waters in half. He scuttles from Australia to the Kalahari – not very far away from where she disappeared and at the chocolate coast of Namibia he hurls himself off Africa to meet land again smack in the middle of São Paulo's megopolis.

In early November on this latitude the rains have not yet abated. Further up on the Cape York peninsula roads are still sodden, their red tropical soil bleeding into mires of muck that only the sturdiest Land Rovers can negotiate. November is the beginning of summer, or what passes for summer in the tropics. In actuality the climate is – not counting the rainy season – stupendously regular. Mornings scream their supremacy with thick bright skies and the beach joggers take their multitoned lycra out for twirls along the boardwalk.

Just outside town there is a sign, the metal kind usually erected on highways. TROPIC OF CAPRICORN. In a nearby tree some artist has carved a goat. All the tourists have their photographs taken in front of the brazen highway sign. This latitude marks their spot on the world, dividing the mild tropics from the savage temperate zones.

Sometimes I go hiking in the pockets of jungle which still survive on the Queensland coast. The northern part of the state is part of the thin Equatorial belt that provides the right conditions for rainforest to grow. I go there even though there is nowhere on earth where I am less comfortable. I am afraid of the jungle; afraid of the whispering trees, the vines that turn into snakes, the log that is not a log but a boa constrictor, the blackberry-size bullet ants and the phenomenal oscillations of the night creatures; the owls and hawks, the toads and frogs.

It is a deeply involved universe, in which one organism feeds off another. This is what is so disturbing about the rainforest: density; the inextricability of things. The feeling that the natural world is one which tends not to entropy but toward an involvement which at once traps and makes significance for those involved. Like a family. Things crawling and creeping around each other in a kind of approximation of the love/hate entwinement of the emotions growing between lovers. And still I walk there, in that chaos of photosynthesis, that perpetually twilight universe.

I never believed them before, those stories you hear about when the telephone rings, and people say: *I just knew*. It rings differently, with a malevolence it has never had before. There is an urgency in its voice which shocks you to the depths of your spleen. I had never believed these post-catastrophe anecdotes claiming clairvoyance: *when the phone rang I just knew*.

I had been back once, flying from my perch in the tropics three years ago. This time was different. I wondered if it would all appear to me now as something finished, a completed circle or cycle. And in tracing its outlines, in mapping the contours of this shape, it would finally be over and done with. But then all time is a circle, revolving over and over again, endlessly accessible, and circles are technically endless. And people are only dead, and really lost forever, when you can no longer hear their voices inside your head.

In that city I discovered sex, mint-green *More* brand cigarettes, and the sudden popularity of knitted ponchos. I was eight years old and wore a lime-green halter top. When I went to the Valu-Fair, ostensibly to get my grandmother nasal decongestant, I was in fact stealing cigarettes and concealing them underneath the poncho, whose fashionability proved useful for shoplifting. I and my juvenile-delinquent-in-training friends smoked on top of the concrete feet of the electricity pylons and in the staircase, which reeked of piss and was punctuated by narrow hallways with strangers ranged on either side. The women who lived in the building were groggy. Babies seemed to be always dying of crib death.

'The women are all Valium junkies, that's why,' my grandmother snapped.

Next door to our apartment building lived a 'Navy' family, as Grandma called them. The father came home in white and stripes, the mother hung clothing out on the washline, and the boys shaved their hair within an inch of their skull. The boys were already rapists at age twelve. I knew to keep away from them, if I could. To get to school I had to cross a catwalk suspended over four lanes of traffic. At the other end, the older boys waited for their prey as we came out of the thin neck of the catwalk like sheep herded through the throat of pastures and into pens.

It was a rented welfare apartment in the harbour district, a geography of Valu-Fairs, dentists' waiting rooms and the four-lane highway between our apartment and my school. My grandmother had taken us there like an advance party, waiting for Bridget's rearguard action to show up. Her letters assured my grandmother that she was coming back any day now. In any case it was a good five hours away from him, and he could not know where we were. So, for the first time since I could remember, I slept straight through the nights, one after the other, unmolested by a nocturnal cacophony of crashes and yells.

The city had an eastern sky, continually lowering with the threat of rain, and weather that changed as effortlessly as my moods. It was a kind of northern equivalent of Dar es Salaam where the interlocking fingers of clouds squeezed the last sun out of the sky, as the oil tankers and oil rigs rusted in the harbour. Even the long summer evenings were no respite. You would hear the drugged-out women in neighbouring apartments fill the building with the off-key D-minor of their moans as the mauve light slipped incrementally from the sky.

Nearly two years had passed since we had left the island when one afternoon I came home from school to find her in our living room, reading a letter.

'What is it?'

'Go away, Morag.'

'I'm not going away until you tell me.'

'All right, then, since you're bent on knowing. It's from Bridget.'

Bridget had written to us every few months, and in each letter she promised that she was returning soon. Each letter told us that she could not get away, not right then. I didn't really know what the letters said, as my grandmother would not let me read them.

She looked up at me. I saw that a big crow had dunked itself into those frozen graphite pools of her eyes.

'She's not coming back.'

'What?'

She took off her glasses and wiped them with a Kleenex. She looked again at me, her shortsighted eyes exposed, their extraordinary stone colour bright in the early morning sun that flooded into the rented apartment. It was spiked with possible meanings, her regard; it was the look, received at the moment of orgasm, from a lover who is free of any tenderness.

'Not ever?'

'I don't know.' Grandma's voice trailed off until it was just a whisper. 'She won't say. She just says she doesn't foresee coming back right now. She's sent some money.'

My grandmother looked back at the hippopotamus on the photograph Bridget had included in her letter, its idiot-savant face. Such creatures, she must have thought. Almost dinosaurs. And her daughter was living amongst them. Would not this alone make her crazy? Who could be surrounded by such threat masquerading as significance and not be affected?

I looked at the deer-and-Jesus velour paintings on the wall. They came with the apartment.

'Well, that means we're doomed to these fucking paintings for the rest of our lives and if you don't mind I'd rather die.'

'What's the matter with those paintings anyway?' She swivelled her head to look up at them. 'I like them.'

I looked again at the paintings. The deer were majestic, triumphant in their antlered haloes. Jesus looked a bit drab, as if he had been faded by the sun.

The river was high that year. Storms carried the rainy season on their backs, moving off to the eastern horizon with the stately pace of colonial era dowagers. It was nearing the end of the rains, and sun filtered through the clouds' satin hems. At night the sky was one half dark, the other light, as the electrical storms advanced south and east towards Zimbabwe.

Hippos, near-invisible in the dark, lazed about in the red-streaked twilight of the river. The sun sank until it was a series of carmine ribbons laid across the cusp of the sky. The river has a frequency embedded in her aural memory. It is like the insistent rhythms of the Gaelic waulking songs of the Hebrides, which women would sing while waulking a piece of raw cloth soaked with cow's urine. The song and its reedy frequency were part of a ritual older than these peoples inhabiting one of the earth's true rims, the Outer Hebrides. Cow's urine, cloth and song and a woman somewhere out there in the vast viscous continent, sitting by an evening river listening to its own song, surrounded by a tribal significance which is forever inaccessible to her.

'You're developing,' she said.

'Into what?' I asked her, heart pounding. She squinted at me, wondering at my sudden stupidity.

'Into a woman.'

I woke up one morning and was transformed into a cow ready for the slaughterhouse, blood dripping from the invisible knives carving me up from the inside out. Some sort of awful black, wiry hair – like little gleaming snakes – was nestling in the warm, entangled spots of my body, covering me in a dense black pelt. I was becoming a wolf. So that was it, I thought: the werewolf has gotten me after all.

I looked at my grandmother's great, heaving breasts, boulders contained within their 'harness' as she lovelessly referred to her mail-order brassiere. Without it, they would sink down to her pubis. 'My breasts used to be normal-sized, until I had your mother,' she said, flinching when she realizes that she had said 'your mother.'

'You mean I'm turning into you?'

'In a manner of speaking.'

'Oh, my God,' I breathed. 'I'd rather die.'

'All girls your age want to die. You go right ahead,' she said nonchalantly. 'I did the best I could.'

Snapshot: Bridget in Rhodesia, soon to become Zimbabwe. Mid-to-late seventies. She wears corduroy trousers where the knees have been rubbed smooth or mini-skirts which somehow seem inappropriate in my grandmother's eyes. She wears spectacles and often poses beside vehicles and her body language speaks of a sense of purpose, of being in the moment. That she is in Africa is not a bid for youthful romanticism. She is simply a long, long way away in an unimaginable landscape that is rendered only slightly more improbable by the rendering of wild unbearable colours on the blank walls every night. There are green monkeys frolicking by the roadside, screeching at Bridget's approach and heading for the highest branches, to swing overhead where they dangle like overripe fruit.

The stupendous excesses of Idi Amin and the mistakes of the single-party socialist-minded governments of Kaunda and Nyerere are yet to be exposed. The whites have begun to leave Rhodesia. The Development Decade is about to begin. Africa, of the faded pink Coca-Cola signs and peeling billboards that depicted scenes and styles already five years out of date in Lisbon, London, Paris. Of the white-bellied dragonflies of aeroplanes – TAP, Lufthansa, British Airways – disgorging possible Bridgets into the stupefying heat and then taking them away again.

She made the mistake of referring to her as my mother.

'SHE'S NOT MY MOTHER,' I yelled.

My grandmother looked up, surprised for once.

'Well,' she said, pursing her lips. 'Aren't you taking after you-know-who.'

'She's not MY MOTHER,' I screamed, again.

My grandmother got out of the rocking chair and came over to me, planting both her arms on either side of me like a lover or an assassin.

'And if she's not,' she posited, coolly, 'then who is?' She pulled back. 'Who do you think you are? Christ? You are not the arbiter of reality, my girl.'

In her posture and her regard she had a resplendent, nearly mathematical certainty, a fusion of an osprey eagle, the huntress Diana, and Pythagoras. She was impressive, like a stone sculpture. It made me want to smash her.

'Don't you think you're going to tell me how things are,' she said, shining in the moment, gathering herself for her final salvo.

'I already knew what was what when you didn't even exist in your mother's wildest dreams.'

I fell asleep, tumbling into the familiar canvas of the familiar dream.

We are at the trailer. My grandmother says, 'Morag, this is your mother.'

I stand facing her, stupid in my snowsuit. Bridget is like a painting, her skin brown, her eyes cornflowers, shouting blue! blue!, her mouth bleeding red. Gold dances in her hair as it does on the lake in the evening.

'Hello.'

'Hello.'

It is a meeting like any other. This is not Judgement Day. My mother goes away again, and everything is as it was before.

'Morag,' Grandma says, fidgeting with her apron, standing grey-skinned against my colouring-book mother.

'This is your mother.'

Then there are dreams of my mother oiling my feet. Her sturdy fingers running along my bones. Dipping my feet into a basin of painfully hot water; red plastic. Like an amniotic fluid. I was there then, swimming and washing around. And she took my feet and the oil and rubbed it into them; my wounded feet.

I tried to see her face, I turned my head toward her face but my face was sluggish, as big and stony as an ox.

My mother's face is very delicate. A long, straight nose, as beautiful as any I have seen, pale blue eyes, a thinnish but well-formed mouth; delicate but strong cheekbones. She has the inoffensively perfect face of a china doll when pale, or of an adventuress when tanned. She is everything and anything she wants to be, because she is so beautiful.

Her beauty seemed to be one of the keys to the room in which great strapping pieces of slaughtered rainforest wood furniture were piled: mahogany escritoires, teak wardrobes, stocky commodes. This is the furniture of Bridget's heart. These things are heavy, yet she carries them everywhere with her. In their locked drawers are stacks of skin-thin papers. And on those faded pieces of parchment are written, in code, the reasons why I would never know her.

The next day I got my first period. Much later I learned that menstruation can be induced by the soaking of feet in hot water.

TWENTY-TWO

A FTER a certain point we did not hear from Bridget again. Until then she sent cards, rather than letters. The cards were always postmarked somewhere in Africa or Greece. And then one year they just stopped. My grandmother phoned the External Affairs Office. They did not have enough to go on. She phoned the RCMP. They said it was out of their jurisdiction. She phoned the local MP, who had a friend who had once worked in the South African consulate. She phoned priests. They said they would pray for her. Cards kept arriving that said Franciscan Friars or Dominican Monks or just plain Catholic Priests were praying for her in the Vatican, at Mount Athos, at St Patrick's cathedral on Fifth Avenue. It was nice to know a Franciscan Friar somewhere was thinking of us, but it didn't do us much good, not really.

My grandmother was out cleaning other people's houses. Then we went on welfare for a while, until Bridget started sending us money from untraceable postes restantes. Two years later she stopped.

The island was five hours away by road but gradually it became five years away, nearly ten. Then it disappeared altogether, taking with it the rust-red blood of the clay soil, the footprints of the Micmacs, and the wild skies sucked backward by the power of the northwesterlies.

The horses, the chickens, the pigs and the sheep disappeared without remorse, as did the endless cadavers of the summer hay

bales, scattered over the mauve-yellow fields. As did the deep
blue gut of water through which licorice-coloured whales slid.

There were pavements now and shopping malls and the concrete pylons of the harbour suspension bridges holding the two
halves of the city together. We could see the twin bridges from
our apartment window: two saurian monsters, their feet planted
resolutely on each side of the harbour, a constant bloodrushing
flow of traffic bleeding back and forth, back and forth.

The jungle of women needed careful negotiation. Particularly
deadly were the Valium Women, always mentally wandering off
to leave their babies. But the real mamba or cobra was the two-
headed monster of my grandmother and I, peering at each other
from across the living room of our apartment, each of us thinking:
who are you?

'You're a smart mouth and a tomboy,' she snapped. 'If you
don't watch out you'll be queer.'

'That's what they said about you and your sisters.'

'Who? Who said that?'

'I don't remember. They meant you were weird, I guess.'

'They meant more than that.'

'What does queer mean then?'

'That's not for me to say.'

'Then how am I gonna find out?'

'You're doing well in school. If you're so smart you can damn
well look it up in a book,' she said.

'I saw her on the sidewalk, you know,' I told her.

She squinted at me. 'Who?'

'My mother.'

My grandmother pursed her lips.

'I stopped to talk to her.'

'Who?'

Had she forgotten already? What was the matter with her?

'My mother.'

'Oh. Morag,' she said, her voice suddenly small and tremulous. 'Don't go daft on me. I need you too much.'

It was a hallucination, of course, just as I had had in the Big House coming down the staircase every morning, the animal with the body of a snake and the teeth of piranhas following at my heels.

'Your grandmother's your mother,' phantom-Bridget said, when I met her on the sidewalk.

'Forget about me,' she said.

And so we learned to hate each other, my grandmother and I, like shipwreck survivors or lost explorers who begin to detest one another's presence.

'You're a Catholic,' she reminded me. 'You get what you deserve.'

'Do people who aren't Catholic get what they deserve too?'

'No,' she said. 'They get what they get.'

The year I was fifteen my grandmother went back to the island. She was finished by then, or nearly; too many years of welfare and cleaning other people's houses; too many years of waiting. I wasn't waiting anymore; I lived with friends for the last two years of high school and then I went away to university. After that, I never thought about the apartment I had shared with my grandmother again.

She had heard my grandfather was living in North Sydney; maybe Glace Bay. In any case, she didn't see him and she didn't want to know. She went back to her sisters, and they all lived together again, just as they had done when they were children and men were a distant threat hovering on their individual horizons.

Maryanne and Jessie's house had always been her second home, as it had been mine. Even if it had always been unnerving. Nobody would go downstairs in the middle of the night, even though the bathroom was there. Everyone used the chamber pots, carrying them down in the morning, the pee sploshing their fingers.

The house was haunted, of course. Jessie's husband had died there, as had my great-grandmother and grandfather. But whatever was wrong with that house seemed older than that; it was as if the ground upon which it stood was uneasy. We could never look out of the windows in the middle of the night, for fear of seeing the wide white, red-ringed eyes of a half-man half-beast staring back at us. Something was out there: there had been sightings of werewolves in the woods by local teenagers, but of course they were likely to be drunk.

'Maryanne had a child who was born dead in that house,' my grandmother said when I brought it up, as if that explained it all.

I tried to visualize it. Aunt Maryanne: saggy-limbed and rasp-voiced by the time I knew her, but red-lipsticked, plump and laughing in the old pictures, the dead bag of baby flesh being pulled out from between her legs, the ominous silence, her bloated body sinking to the bottom of an unfathomable ocean as it recognizes what has happened.

'A dead thing came out of me,' Maryanne screams. 'A dead thing came out from between my legs.'

Later, the priest would comfort her. 'That was your son, Maryanne. He's with God now, he's an angel. It wasn't a thing. It was your son. We'll bury him tomorrow. I've baptized him. He will rest in peace with our Lord and Saviour.'

'A dead thing. Its flesh already rotting. Oh Jesus, the devil was inside me. I've given birth to the devil.'

Her screams go on for hours, until the priest can't stand it anymore. He calls for the doctor.

'Give her Valium. Give her anything, but for the love of God make her shut up.'

In the morning the child is buried in a tiny grave on the hillside overlooking Boisedale, on the south side of the island. It is a windy autumn day. The weather has changed already, and frost is travelling down from the Arctic to settle in for its long winter visit.

As the priest puts the box into the ground – no bigger than a shoebox, but fortified so that the wolves can't open it if they manage to dig it up – a strong gale comes out of nowhere. The mourners have to fight to keep their footing, and from a distance they look like dark frayed sheets of washing hung out on the line, rippling in the wind.

'And then there was Jessie's child,' she continued.

'What?'

'She had a child by a man who you wouldn't know,' she recalled. 'He was married. That was all a long time ago. But then it was born dead too.'

Another dead child. But that didn't explain the wolfman in the hall, in the blue room where I slept, the quivering hairy beast who stood upright on fabulously muscled legs and eyed me from pupil-less orbs. Nor did it explain the other horrendous nightmares. Or the fear of the house at night.

'You don't know the half of it.' She shook her head, as if in pity. Meaning, I had no idea what went on in the sexual lives of these people I thought I knew so well.

'There are things people do not divulge,' she said. 'Not even to their own children.'

I looked at her. She had always been my ally. Why was she dissociating herself from me, simply because I was growing up?

I thought these women knew so little about sex and the Ways of the World – I thought their awareness extended only to the fact that they were fought over but simultaneously undervalued, like Poland, doomed to a totalitarian future under the triumvirate of tyrannies of Wife, Mother, and Lover.

In retrospect, a new world was opening. It was a cruel version of the place I thought had been home. I wondered what other things my grandmother had kept from me.

The banishing from the Highlands and Islands spawned not

anger, perversely, but a culture of shame. When I was young it was not discussed – exactly how we came to be on the island.

'You don't want to know about that,' my grandmother or one of the other women would say. 'It'll only make you sad.'

Like women who have been raped, they would not talk about it. They just shut their eyes tightly and waited for whatever memory was cantering toward them to go away. Repressing the need to cry out or to hit out is like repressing the need for sex, as if it is a humiliation to want these things.

The land, the land.

They cried over it as though they could have suckled their children on its milk-thick sweetness, even though it was tough and dry as an old tit.

I saw a woman and a child crying and screaming as they were put on the boat . . .

It is a fear that carries itself down through the ages, like a gene defect: fear of leaving narcotically entwined with dreams of leaving. Because many people wanted to go, yes. Life was hard. But they did not want to be compelled to go. Much less did they want to be betrayed by their own people. It was their own who banished them, who cared no more for them than they did for sheep.

It was a dark shame; floating just beneath the meniscus of history and story and folklore, like the whale I once saw from a plane as we banked into Brisbane, passing beneath the surface of the sun-struck water, heading up to the Great Barrier Reef.

So that generations later, the act of leaving can still seem like a banishment. And the Garden of Eden, though strewn with stones and serpents, is missed as if it had been a tender lover, and not someone who had been trying all along to kill you.

This leaving by night and suddenly, we do it only when there is nothing more to be done.

Bridget drove Land Rovers across swollen rivers and through rutted ground. She flew a small single-engined plane up to

Lusaka, or down into the Okavango, where she could see herds of antelope travelling like flocks of birds against the red and green sky-ground of the Delta. She hitchhiked to Dar es Salaam and felt the pure unadulterated power and the roar as she stood at the edge of Victoria Falls. She stayed on the blighted continent because foreigners can fall in love with places whose tribulations can never really touch them.

She liked the savagery of it, its removal from her. It was at least as savage as her father. And it was this continent that ate her up whole, sweet and fresh, like a mango, a papaya, or other unknowable fruit, the continent that swallowed her as a whale would swallow a slippery helpless oyster, and then spit out its pearls.

I do not know any of this for sure. I only know what I know from her slides, and the sound of heat, my imagined sound. The swish and hum, swish and hum. The oars dipping into the soup of the river in a syncopated rhythm. The wash of the water against the boat. Hulks of thick clouds advancing from the west. The sky to the south clear, a brownish-blue reflecting the far-off face of the Kalahari.

Snapshot: Bridget, a slim woman in a silk skirt under a palm tree. It seems as if I have never looked at a photograph that hasn't contained that woman lurking, invisible to everyone but me, in the background.

In all those sad tales from Barra and Uist women are left behind, pregnant by men who will never stay with them. And still the women insist upon the loveliness of it all, looking out to sea and singing their songs of remorse. The men never do. *I don't want to know you*, they say. Or they say cleverer things like: *I have no expectations*. And they walk forward into the blinding promise of a new morning, of a new woman, of which they are an infinite supply growing like blueberries on the glowing August rims of their futures.

*   *   *

She would not give him any more children, only Bridget, her one and only preternaturally beautiful daughter.

Nor would Olympias give Philip of Macedon another son, for fear of jeopardizing the succession of Alexander, of her beloved first-born.

Be true to yourself, the oracle instructs men.

Be true to your children, is the prophecy for women.

I had to give up on women. They are always disappearing, trading their women's secrets among one another. Their histories are so much more raucous and bloody than men's, no matter how much blood a violent drunken man or a Macedonian king can draw.

I had spent too much time in the woods with bullets heavy in my palms. It seemed certain, the transformation; that I would turn into him. Everybody always hinted at it: *she's so like her grandfather. Such a temper. Such a good shot.*

I didn't want any of it. Not to be him, not to be a woman. In the end I couldn't avoid it, the transformational code imprinted inside me. And so I became one, the women who are made only to disappear, either to far-off island continents, or into the heads of their children, so chock-full of dancing mother shadows there can be no room for any other meaning.

TWENTY-THREE

H<small>E</small> opened the door.
    'What did I ever do to you?' was the first thing he asked me.

His face had turned feral, I saw. What had made it like that? He opened the door wider, and I passed through.

The year I was sixteen I found him in Sydney Mines. He hadn't been seen in any of his usual haunts and as far as we knew he had stopped playing anything, from violin to guitar to accordion. Nobody had seen him at any house parties, no one had run into him in the Mall. Although she rarely spoke of him, my grandmother began to worry, and so I came back from the city. I was dispatched, my new driver's licence in hand, to track him down. It hadn't been very hard to find him. A visit to one of his cousins had done the trick.

Sydney Mines used to be a coal-mining town – coal seams were scattered all through the Appalacians, just as copper and aluminium sprout from the heel of the Andes and as emeralds line the oesophagus of Queensland. Most of the mines were closed by then. From his bedroom window he could see the abandoned mine, its iron-rust superstructure tilting now like a dinosaur skeleton in a bombed-out museum.

It was a three-room apartment at the end of a long hallway paved with chipped linoleum and surrounded by women screaming at their children, or husbands, or boyfriends. He shared a kitchen with a man named Donald who was sick and dying and who smelt sour and whose bedroom stunk of bitter-salt piss. He took care of Donald, got his medicines, changed his bedpan. There sure as hell wasn't anyone else who was going to do it. He had a squeaky spring bed and a room that overlooked Main Street in Sydney Mines.

'What cause did you have to just leave me there? You don't love me,' he wagged his cigarette at me. 'I was going to leave everything I had to you. But now you've mauled your future, my girl.'

It was not diminished, the tone of him, not even by a minor third; as if the night we had left was only last night. The tone of myself, too, was the same. They were both set in a minor key, descending like the bog songs of the Highlanders into the voluptuousness of regret.

'What the fuck are you on about?'

'Don't you fuck with me,' he said. 'Nor use me neither. I loved you with all my heart and you just spit on it. Now you won't get a cent and you can go cry in your hat.'

Yellow light from the streetlights slanted in the window. Across the street was a fish and chip shop and pool parlour where men with multiple tattoos and greasy baseball caps hung out until the small hours. In his room was a small television with my picture propped up on top of it. He had a stack of *Maclean's* and a stack of *Reader's Digests* and some books I had sent him, many about the war, on a rickety old bookcase. In a green plastic suitcase he kept his prosthesis, a consequence of his latest cancer. He now had no bladder; just a hole in his side through which a single plastic tube was fed. Another smaller suitcase was full of photographs. His clothes took up three small drawers and two cardboard boxes.

A blue house. Late afternoon in December.

'Morag.' He said my name as if he had never uttered it before. 'Who are you?'

I knew he didn't have amnesia. He was really asking who I was.

'I'm you.'

And he smiled in the perpetual dusk of the room, while Donald rolled over, the bedsprings and his voice together in a symphony of moaning.

'Are you?' He smiled. This is what he wanted to hear. 'Can you tell me who I am?'

'Yes, Grandpa.'

'Don't abuse me,' he warned. 'She took you away from me,' he said. I did not know who he was talking about: Christine, or Bridget.

'You took me away from her,' I reminded him.

'I love you more than my life,' he says.

'Yeah, yeah, yeah.' I shove my hands into my pockets.

'Cut out that juvenile delinquent posture.'

'Do you know where I learned that?'

'I just loved you.' He ignores me. 'From the first second I saw you.'

I nod, miserably. I know. I have heard of love at first sight.

It was there like bauxite in the steel seams of the island's stomach, ready to be mined, inexhaustible; his love. He had just loved me in his simplicity. *It was almost unnatural. The way he loved you. As if you had been put on this earth to save him.*

It is too much of a burden, all this love crashing down from someone who swears that the only person who can save him is you – you who are neither daughter nor lover nor wife. It was a dumb love, an albatross's insane allegiance to the egg that waits, five thousand kilometres away, for its return.

I looked around me like a fugitive, looking for an escape. It was getting hot in the room, stifling. All I wanted to do was get out. It's cruel, I know. There's this man in front of me who lives to see me. Literally, I keep him alive. Or so he tells me. And all I want to do is to be anywhere – really anywhere – else.

I am a court intriguer, one of those stooping acolytes who are clever enough never to affect an unctuous manner. My destiny is inextricably linked with that of the king. It was true that I had needed subtleties of this calibre, just to get through the minutes with him. I thought: *You'll regret this hunted posture you adopt, these marshmallow compromises.* Simultaneously I thought: *You'll be guilty when he's dead and no one else will love you this way again.*

We sat in the room above Main Street, Sydney Mines. A forlorn town, like a hungover barfly, waiting for the prosperity that never came, washed up on the industrial suds of the Atlantic, the core of its black heart mined out. In December, young men rush from the pool hall, throw themselves in the cabs of their pickup trucks, and roar around the corner to catch the liquor store before closing time.

'Got you some lobster,' he smiled.

'How the hell did you get a fresh lobster in December?'

'Oh, I have my ways. Got a friend at the airport.'

'How's a guy at the airport going to help you?'

'Flown in from Jamaica,' he said smoothly, holding his punchline suavely to the last.

And there it was, a Jamaican lobster. It was like bringing coals to Newcastle. Our lobster was among the best in the world, but then it was out of season now. The Jamaican lobster was probably destined for some expensive Sydney restaurant or businessman's banquet.

'Ours not to reason why,' he shrugged.

His singlet was tattered at the edges and his trousers hung open where he had not bothered to belt them. I could see the lip of his prosthesis sticking out from above the band of his underpants.

I looked in the fridge. A tub of yoghurt. A bit of ham, some boiled cabbage covered with Saran wrap. A plastic container of soup.

'Do you get enough to eat, Grandpa?' I looked over to the table to where he sat rolling a cigarette, waiting for my lobster to boil. He was licking the edge of his rolling paper. When he had finally pressed it down he looked up at me to answer my question. I began to cry.

'There, there.' Donald blew my nose. He had materialized out of nowhere. It was the first time I had seen him out of bed.

'There, there,' Donald said again, looking much more cheerful.

The lobster boiled, and we shared it. Donald's rickety legs poked out beneath the table. We pushed the rolling papers and the tin of tobacco away and set down some newspaper to catch the juice.

'Jamaican, you say?' asked Donald thoughtfully. 'It's a damn good lobster,' he affirmed, smacking what was left of his teeth. 'Them clippers travel fast these days. Did you get some rum off the boat too?'

My grandfather and I exchanged glances. Donald was quite *compos mentis*, but definitely moored in another century. My grandfather winked at me as he broke open a claw with his bare hands.

'They gave me EST, the bastards.'

'What's that?'

'Electroshock therapy,' he said. 'Totally unnecessary in my case. All it does is fry your brain. That's what they do to the poor bastards who they haven't got a clue about. As to what's wrong with them, I mean.'

He flicked his ash into the tray. He wasn't supposed to be smoking anymore, now that he had throat cancer. But he seemed to have given up the fight. His stay in the loony bin had taken it out of him. In comparison with before, he now seemed strangely passive. And this was the worst crime they had perpetrated: they had taken the fight out of him.

No one had told me where he was in those missing eight years. When he made the same five-hour trip as she and I had travelled, he made it in the back of an ambulance. He had gone down at Maryanne and Jessie's, down on the floor, writhing like a snake on fire, sweat in his hair and sea-foam on the corners of his lips.

Drugs and alcohol; a bad combination, but not one to make you crazy. At the hospital they shocked the split in his light blue eyes – the axis on which his person would revolve, now Jekyll, now Hyde – so that it went spinning right outside of him. So that it was gone, finally, the drive toward destruction that I had seen twisting around inside him like the slow scrape of the glacier across the continent. Also gone was the dangerous light in his eyes flickering with the delicacy of grace notes – the same look he always had when he played.

On the bed he jumped and leaped like a silverfish in the sea. He popped up and down like popcorn in a pot. His nerves lashed out like a cat-o'-nine tails. Finally he came to rest, a survivor of a shipwreck, washed up on a calm sandy beach.

'The first thing I saw,' he told me later, 'was a young woman running naked down the hall screaming. She wasn't much older than yourself, Morag.'

He looked at me steadily, as if he were giving me a warning that I too could easily become a young naked woman running down the corridor of a mental hospital.

'Initially,' he recalled, 'I thought I might have been crazy. That's sure as hell what it felt like. But as soon as they wheeled me in *that* place, BANG!' he said, and he slapped his hands on his knees, 'I knew I was saner than any of them Jesus psychiatrists they got in there.

'There were no fewer than five guys in white coats running after her,' he smiled to himself. 'Each one brandishing a strait-jacket. By God, she could run,' he said admiringly. And then his eyes clouded over.

After he came out of there, he really wasn't the same.

'You take some poor guy like me,' he continued. 'From out in the middle of nowhere. Makes a mistake and goes a bit funny. Has a nervous breakdown. So they ship him to that insane asylum and fry his brain.

'Do you know how I feel?' he asked, his cigarette hand shaking. 'I feel like I've been all jumbled up inside. Like I used to be a jigsaw puzzle that had been put together. Maybe there were a lot of pieces, but at least it was holding. And now I'm all scattered. And nobody will ever be able to put me right again. You know that nursery rhyme?' he asked. ' "Humpty Dumpty sat on a wall. Humpty Dumpty had a great fall." And all the King's horses and all the King's men were about as much fucking use as a legion of drunken Highway Maintenance crew guys on a Saturday night. I couldn't even begin to think which piece of myself went where.'

We sat there in that apartment above Main Street, Sydney Mines. It was a winter afternoon, and the light slanted in at a skewed, oriental angle through his apartment window, turning everything, including my grandfather's face and the tears that made their meandering course down his quilted and mottled skin, a peculiar glowing orange.

TWENTY-FOUR

THE next time I saw him was the following year, the night the house burned down. He called me in the city and I drove the five hours to the island in record time.

That night the island was set aglow like Dresden. It wasn't him, I knew that. Although the RCMP thought otherwise. He was drunk when they arrested him. I had to go to Sydney Mines to bail him out. I explained the house was no longer ours; we had no insurance claims upon it. All our things were burnt down with the house, valueless things, like the books his mother used to take to read in the long winter lumber camp nights.

Finally, the RCMP were satisfied that he had no Motive.

'Take care of your grandpa,' they said as they stepped out of the station.

'You bet.' I hauled my grandfather's arm over my shoulder so that I could drag him to the car.

'I only ever loved you; you were my sweetheart.'

'Yeah, yeah, yeah.' I was seventeen years old. The last thing I wanted was to be anybody's sweetheart.

He slobbered on my neck.

'You're overly ardent this evening.' I pushed him off and laid him gently in the passenger seat. I was joking, but of course I was burning. I got in the car and turned the ignition key.

'It was arson,' he said.

'What?' I couldn't hear him. He was mumbling.

'Ardour,' he said, drooling on the passenger seat as I drove. 'It was ardour.'

He was drunk. Arson and ardour: near enough sonorically.

Ardour, from the old French: *to burn.*

The chimney and the water tank, painted green our last summer together, were all that remained. The alders and the scrub-brush and the long grass moved in to reclaim the charred ground.

The plum tree died; the old apple tree was scorched and never recovered. People came from miles around to see the house burn. Somebody called my grandfather in Sydney Mines and he jumped in the car and drove like a demon. The fire brigade took an hour to arrive, and by that time he had grabbed a gun from the back of his car and was tracking the arsonists. Only he didn't get too far; all he had to go on were the burned rubber tyre tracks pulling out of the driveway.

Shortly afterwards he was picked up by the RCMP.

Then shalt thou be pleased with the sacrifices of righteousness, with burnt offering and whole burnt offering? When all is dead and gone, and all testimony to those who lived and loved, toiled and worked, slept and ate and drank, is burnt?

Then someone called me. I never saw the house burn. I was seven hours too late for that, although the charred embers were still smoking like a morning campfire when I arrived.

And then I had to bail him out of the jail. Possession of firearms out of season. They suspected he would have shot them, but how can you track tyre marks on asphalt? They drove away, to points unknown.

Then shalt thou be pleased, Lord?

A vengeful Lord, yes.

The smell of fire fresh on my face. As if I had been to an effigy burning. I saw it on television; it was in Iran. As if I had been to the powwows my grandfather used to take me to at the reservation. Or to one of the summer parties, that last summer on the island, the dancing, the roast wieners, the periwinkle boils we had had on the beach, the midnight driftwood fires by the shore.

She is seventeen, this girl who is also me, and she bends down and fingers the still-warm earth, the ash and the black carbon, crouching down to touch the ground where the ashes of the toys and the mahogany cabinets and the great-grandmother's spinning wheel intermingle. The grass is still charred around the Big House where the flames reached below the floorboards.

She feels animal, as if she could speak to the bears who watch her from the woods. She feels spooked. When she stands up her face is streaked with dirt. She has painted her face with the soil and the charcoal has sunk into her skin. Black lines are criss-crossed on her cheeks, her forehead. She is a warrior crawling through the same undergrowth centuries back, before the coming of the lentil-faced whitemen.

The Lord is sleeping unawares and his guard is down.

She is in that country again, the one in which only what she does defines who she is. She draws the boundaries of what she will do and so she draws the boundaries of herself. But the lines never quite come together; they are the endless frontier, longer than the Pacific rim.

Later that night, after the ground had stopped smoking, I drove him back to his apartment. We sat there for a long time, our silence punctuated by Donald's moans as he turned himself over in his bed.

It was like a wake. We talked in hushed tones, mainly of the house.

He turned to me. 'Do you remember that wolf we had hanging around that winter?'

In the autumn the wolf had been driven out of the interior by the loggers and deprived of his rabbits. By January he was hungry. He would sit there, looking mournfully at the house. He would never approach us when we came out with food for him. My grandfather put out meat for him so he wouldn't eat our sheep. The wolf was quiet. He never howled. He watched us inquisitively, a look of utter intelligence soldered by hurt.

'The wolf is one of the most misunderstood animals. He is not vicious,' my grandfather had explained to me at the time. 'Not to you or me at least. You should respect the wolf, but don't never fear him. Just give him a wide berth and he won't hurt you. He's shy. If you throw a stone at him he'll only slink away.'

I had seen him do this in the morning, the wolf going off to hunt, nose to the snow with his hunched posture of the unloved.

In the evening I would watch him from the window of their second-floor bedroom. I could just see his black silhouette, a dark inkblot on a piece of white paper as he sat there in the field of snow. When the moon came out, he sprang into relief like a piece of silver tinsel caught by the light on a Christmas tree.

'Look at him,' my grandfather said from behind me where I stood at the window. 'Tsk tsk,' he clicked his tongue. 'Such a lonely bugger, the poor thing.'

We watched the wolf approach the meat suspiciously, as if it were a snake about to lunge at him.

My grandfather spoke. 'I bet his ancestral memory is telling him to be careful, that the meat might be poisoned. There were lots of them who misunderstood the wolf,' he explained. 'They thought he was dangerous so they poisoned him just like that, setting out meat for him to gnaw on when he was cold and hungry. Then they'd watch him die of stomach convulsions.'

In the apartment on Main Street my grandfather sighed. 'Some of us are called to be alone.'

I only rolled my eyes. 'I wish you'd shut up about destiny and drink the beer I bought you.'

'You're special, you know.' He ignored me. 'Because you were born out of wedlock. You were a bastard.'

'So I should be shot up with sensuality,' I sighed. 'I guess I should be unnerving while I'm at it.'

I knew his game by then: he wanted to teach me to love

anything that was fierce and to eschew all contact with the soft creatures of the world who had been too deeply stamped with their own reality.

'Now there's no need to go all sarcastic.' He pursed his lips.

'You can't expect me to just take everything you say as Gospel anymore, Grandpa.'

'I never said I did.' He flicked his ash into the ashtray, avoiding my eyes. 'I just expected you to give me a fair hearing. Don't you think we thought any less of you just 'cause your father didn't want you. We might have been lots of things but weren't the judgemental type. I know it's not easy,' he said. 'Coming from nowhere.'

'You mean Cape Breton?'

'No, of course I don't mean Cape Breton. *Here's* where it's at. Out there ...' he gestured, sweeping his arm toward the window '... out there they're only pretending they're somewhere. All those poor buggers caught in the cities. No, I meant nowhere as in you don't have anybody to tell you who you are.'

'I still have you two.'

'No.' He shook his head slowly, thoughtfully. 'I don't think you do.'

'Well,' I tried another tack. 'I have her photographs.'

It was true. I had all those slides, their thick Kodachrome colours of Victoria plum-juice reds, caramel yellows, the loam of mahogany browns – hues that existed before film processing colours became washed out and effaced like the Valium women in the apartment block who brought children into the world so that they could die.

'No.' He shook his head firmly, his hair still black, still lustrous, reining in the light of the single kitchen bulb. 'I don't think you've had those either. Not since that night.'

In the kitchen he goes on. He rambles in a way he never used to before.

'Inside us, there is nothing but death, ticking away,' he

explains. 'So we're angry. Who wants to be a creature tied to a time bomb?' He turns his eyes, now watery, distilled of their psychosis, towards me.

'It's like being shackled for life to your eventual betrayer,' he explains. 'That's why we kill, you see. That's what the hunting and the fishing and the trapping is all about. Sure, it's survival. But it's also an attempt to pay back that sneering clock.'

He exhausts me. I have trouble following his ellipses. I wonder, now, did he always have this skewered articulation, so beyond his breeding, his education, his experience?

'And you'll never die,' he lies to me. 'You've got to fight the bastard. As long as you're fighting to stay alive, you'll never die.'

'Why?' I ask. 'Is there some special section of immortality reserved for stubborn people?'

He draws his lips back. 'Now you've gone and spoiled it. I was going to tell you a story.'

'Well, go on, tell it anyway. Don't pay any attention to me.'

'No.' He shakes his head petulantly. 'You just want to make fun of me. You think I'm spouting sentimental claptrap about animals. You listened to that stuff, all those stories that explain the world, when it was Dan who was telling you. Just cause I'm not Indian you think I'm not authentic.'

'Oh, come on, that's not fair. You got me all keyed up to hear the end.'

'Nope.' He shakes his head. 'You've gone and spoiled the story. You know better than me, right? You think they succeeded in frying my brain in that loony bin, don't you? Well.' He stubs out his cigarette with some savagery. 'I'm not going to tell you how it ends,' he says, pleased with himself, his lips set. 'Now you can just go and wonder.'

I do wonder. I perform excavations on myself. They are endlessly tedious. The skeletons you find; the bodies of small animals rotting into the loam. A petrified stone of fermenting fruit – the livid peach, dried of its thick juices. In the ditch grime my field workers are busy dusting off tiny fragments of pottery. Vases have cracked inside me centuries ago. Science has run galloping ahead through my veins. There are one or two brush strokes of Picasso's inside me, masquerading as cell clusters.

Some time in the night, the ship breaks its mooring, and floats loose in the harbour. The gull sits on the back of the water buffalo, whose skin is so thick he cannot feel its feet there, prehensile and brittle as twigs. Whales' whiskers, the thickness of telephone wire, nose the hulls of supertankers, gently investigate the coral-clad wrecks of Spanish galleons in the Bay of Biscay, whispering their message in the songs that have the same frequency as the Highland laments: this is what it means not to be anchored in the world – yes, you can free associate, if you are so inclined. But that won't make you free.

The times in my life I have thought most heavenly, as if I were inhabiting my own skin and not that of an imposter, have in fact been the most hellish. But I felt alive there, always, in that room of assassins – rejection, usury, manipulation, indifference. I was at home in that poisoned country wherein I betrayed myself, and kept betraying myself. When will I ever stop getting heaven and hell mixed up?

I leave him in his flimsy apartment, get in the car and return to my grandmother and my aunts' house. From the car radio and from the radio in Maryanne and Jessie's kitchen pour endless country songs.

> *It's a heartache*
> *Nothin' but a heartache*

The smell of the Atlantic in winter; a fume of oranges and salt-logged wood. Cloves and other spices of Christmas cake. The sour corpses of cranberries.

> *Hits you when it's too late*

The Trans-Canada Highway in the off season, devoid of

tourists and their American automobile flamboyancies. Driving back and forth, back and forth. I could drive this road blindfolded. It's the only thing I know by heart, besides the Country tunes and their frequency of love gone wrong and realization come too late.

> *It's a heartache*
> *Nothin' but a heartache*
> *Hits you when it's too late*
> *Hits you when you're down.*

TWENTY-FIVE

B OSTON was the nearest place to which I could fly reasonably direct. Even then it took nearly twenty-four hours of solid flying. From Boston it seemed simpler just to get the bus north.

We crawled slowly along the coastal road, which was in bad repair and subject to bouts of blinding fog, through the piecemeal states of New England, across the bottom of New Hampshire's thin flint blade, eventually sidling up against the stolid flank of Maine. Maine was where the place names on the green highway signs began to be familiar: *Madawaska, St Andrews, Presque Isle.*

CANADIAN CUSTOMS. ALL FOUR LANES. I could see it, just beyond the border: the Trans-Canada Highway, the long grey ribbon stretched across the continent, moving in a way not much different from the grey vipers I see wiggling across the path where I jog at twilight.

The tundra belt begins not too far north from here, in Newfoundland and Labrador, and as the bus approached the border the turn from autumn to winter became more tangible. The slate-grey water in the mouth of the Bay of Fundy appeared, looking like the back of a giant whale – smooth, glossy, skin-like and undulating in its pure ermine expansiveness. Here the clay sand was ochre, with waterless fissures strewn in the wake of the tidal bore so that the shore had the pleated face of an old woman. Squat forms of oil refineries began to dot the coast, and dark gelatinous seaweed clung to the rocks of the shoreline like blobs of congealed grease.

The leaves had already turned carmine, the colour of blood with too much oxygen. The endless autumn, ticking down its slow montane slope into the yearly temperate zone disintegration. The whole forest on fire, a burning woven carpet of ochres and rusts beaded with the corpses of former berries. I look out the window and see them on the highwayside brambles, just as I remember them from two dozen Octobers and Novembers in the north: the withered wild raspberries, fruit of a searing unnatural sweetness, guarded by thorns.

We left the duty-free shops and the borderland limbo behind and entered the country of rusty gas pumps, salt-grey clapboard houses and old wrecked Ford Falcons in driveways. For hours and hours, all the way from Saint John the only sound I heard was the slide guitar rhythm of bus travel; the grinding down of gears in a steady, almost choral procession – sometimes A flat, sometimes D minor. Flickering faces in passing vehicles registered staccato contact as they flew by on the other side of the road, trapped in their rain-spattered vehicles. They were heading south, no doubt, to the Carolinas and to Florida for lazy days under sycamore trees and empty autumn beaches.

We were approaching the northern extremity of the temperate zone, run up against the sub-polar regions, the ones that show up as mint blue in geographical atlases. Here, we were nailed to the cardinal points of a compass, our heads pointing north, as surely as Christ had been fixed to his cross. Because there was this feeling we had: that somehow the position we occupied on the globe had actually formed us, compositionally, so that we were only the residual memories of glaciers or icebergs and other topographical monstrosities of the north. We had been stewed in the vicissitudes of our given parallel so that we were northerners, and this seemed to mean something inescapable, no matter what ingenious latitude we might later chose for our exile.

I went to the southern hemisphere because I wanted to live somewhere where even the sky was different, where the water went down the drain in the opposite direction. I wanted to live under the Southern Cross and not the continuous cyclops eye of the North Star.

I thought, in going to the other side of the world, I might finally figure out how to identify what was heaven and what was hell, up and down, right and wrong.

It was he who had lodged the idea in my head in the first place, the winter he stole me and we set off driving for Mexico/Australia. He wanted to come, but could never quite get the money together. I think he would have thought it a wonderful place, where people were not made haggard and interior by a long winter, a warm, relaxed, arrogant country where you could make yourself anew. Of course it's not like that. After five years, I know that.

The only time I came back, three years ago, he was still living in the plywood apartment. He lived there alone. Donald had died the previous year.

'Why do you stay here?' I asked him, surveying the cheap vinyl on the floor and the endless twilight of the room. 'It's so depressing.'

'Oh,' he shrugged. 'The Legion's just down the street. Don't have to go far for my grog and my friends. That's all you need when you're my age.'

He looked at me more curiously now, as if the years I had been away had made me a stranger.

'How the hell did you get there?' he asked.

I shrugged. 'I swam.'

'All the way there?' He smiled, but there was no lightness in it. I could already see he wanted a scene.

'Well, I stopped off for a rest in Raratonga and Auckland.' I rolled my eyes. 'Haven't you heard about extended-range 747s?'

'Oh sure,' he drawled. 'I keep good and current. Technology

don't escape me. I was just testing you. See if you think your grandfather's an imbecile, now that you're all grown up and hoity-toity.'

He put one of his cigarette papers through the roll-up machine.

'So how are you keeping there?' He was trying to sound nonchalant.

'All right,' I shrugged. 'Just working.'

'Working, eh? In Australia.' He darted a look at me. 'You come from the richest country in the world. What are you doing going and being an immigrant in somebody else's place?'

He rummaged in his shirt pocket for a cigarette paper. 'You know our ancestors worked their fingers to the bone so that none of their kind would ever have to go through what they went through? And here you are repeating the process. You could have gone to Australia in 1850 with the rest of them. Maybe you would have ended up in the same place now,' he hypothesized, twirling the rolling paper in his fingers, watching me to make sure I was getting his drift. 'We could have been sent on a ship bound for Botany Bay instead of Glace Bay. What did you do, get the two Sydneys mixed up? Sydney, Australia, and Sydney, Cape Breton?'

'They weren't sent to Australia. They went to New Zealand,' I told him. 'Australia was a penal colony.'

'So what's the people like out there, anyway?' he asked.

'Just like anywhere else,' I said. 'Some good, some bad.' I kept my eyes low. I concentrated on the fluttering butterfly pattern of the formica and chrome kitchen table.

'Well.' He shot his eyes up sideways as he lit his cigarette. 'That's history for you. You live through it, apparently, but you still don't understand a Jesus thing. Everybody just scatters and they never come back no more. Lot of fuckin' good history does you.' The smoke drifted up into his eyes. They narrowed. 'You were in such a rush to get out of here I could practically see the dust billowing in your wake.'

He had lost me. I looked up at him, sideways, slanting my eyes carefully as I know I do.

'Oh, don't you worry,' he said breezily. 'I'm not going to make a big production out of it. I'm just wondering. As usual I'm left wondering.'

'Don't feel so sorry for yourself. You're just jealous. You always wanted to go to Australia.'

'Jealous, am I?' He laid his cigarette in the ashtray's teeth and leant across the table at me. 'Well, let me tell you something. I wanted to disappear. I just figured going to Australia was the closest I could get to disappearing without dying. I didn't want to die. That was your grandmother.'

'I'm not dead,' I said. 'And I didn't disappear.' I held out the palms of my hands for him to inspect. 'See?' I said. 'I'm real.'

He looked down at them. 'I can see that.' He picked his cigarette back up and wedged it in the corner of his mouth. 'You look quite alive to me. But that's not much of a love line you've got there. How're you doing for boyfriends?'

'Oh, fuck off.'

He came at me all of a sudden so that I actually flinched. I never flinch.

'What did I ever do to you? What cause did you have to just leave me there? You just went with her,' he spat. 'You just sided with who's ever on top. You go with who's winning.'

'I was eight years old.'

'Don't you have a brain at eight years old?'

'Oh leave me the fuck alone.'

'I sure the fuck won't.' He leant across, stabbing me with his cigarette. 'Not then, not now, not ever. You tell me. You knew what you were doing.'

'Yes,' I conceded. 'But it was the first time I did.'

'Well, you sided with her in the end. After all I taught you.'

'You see everything in sides. We're not a football team.'

'Yes we are, and you do take sides. Do you know why? 'Cause you choose.' He sat back in his chair, satisfied with his outburst, waiting for me to understand. I just looked at him, waiting for the storm to pass.

'You choose this.' His arms shot up, and he flung his hands out to the right. 'Or you choose that,' he said, swooping to the left. Then he leant forward again and fixed me with his glacier eyes. 'That's what's called choosing, and you do it all your life. Everything's a choice. You choose who you're going to love. All this falling in love crap. Falling in love my arse. You might fall in the shit but you sure as hell choose who it is you're going to spend the rest of your life with. We like to kid ourselves it's all just accident. But I know better. You stop dodging responsibility for what you did. You had plenty of choice.'

He squinted at me through the blue smoke. 'I was just fooling around. You knew that. You'd seen me do the same before. She provoked me. Well,' he said, sitting back in the old vinyl chair. 'I hope that decision's kept you good company over the years. Tell me.' He leant forward again. 'Did that decision teach you to shoot? Did it teach you to string up cod nets? Did it love you, did it teach you how to read and write . . .'

'. . . she taught me that . . .'

'I don't give a fuck,' he spat. 'It wouldn't have mattered then. If you'd just left things be.'

'What?' I said.

'What?' he said.

'What wouldn't have mattered.'

'That she never came back,' he shrugged. 'It wouldn't have mattered. I would have provided for you.'

That she never came back. That she intended to leave me there, with him, forever.

'I'd had enough,' I said.

'You were eight years old.' He wagged his cigarette at me. 'Just like you said. Remember? Well tell me, how does an eight-year-old ever know what's enough? I'm sixty-three and I don't have a fucking clue. You only know what's enough when things are through. When they're done. That's what's enough.'

'So you just would have gone on and on.'

'Wrong.' He stabbed his finger at me. '*We* would have gone on and on.' I looked up at him sideways again and I could see he was crying. 'All of us,' he said. 'Together.'

Seeing his tears made me cruel, just like he said I was. I saw his weakness and I went for his throat.

'At eight years old, I couldn't imagine,' I said, leaning across the table, telling him, slowly, deliberately, so that he would never forget nor doubt the authenticity of what I was about to say. 'I couldn't imagine,' I repeated, 'spending one more night in that place. With you.'

That was our last conversation. The next I heard from him was when the telephone rang and its sound was so alarming, so malevolent, I knew that it was him, or, rather, that it was about him.

After the bus disgorged its load in Sydney I rented a car. On the way up to the house I drove down to the spot.

The Big House used to be here, although all that is left is the oil tank. What am I doing standing here all by myself, waiting for the werewolf to get me? There's a funeral I have to go to, about eight miles up the road.

The silence all around. The car is my only company, here beside me with the headlights on, the door left open at a crazy angle. Just as he would park the car when he would pull up on the side of the highway for a piss or to move some animal he had just thumped underneath his wheels.

This piece of ground has no meaning for me, or whatever it once possessed of meaning has floated off with the ashes into the treetops.

But this was my home. Where is everyone? This is my home.

As the light fades early in the November day I turn automatically, like a compass, to face the true north.

TWENTY-SIX

I T happened during one of my infrequent visits to him in the last couple of years before I went to Australia. He had asked me to go back to the trailer and get some things from the shed.

'Oh, come on,' he pleaded. 'Come with me. You can just stay outside while I get the things. You don't have to come in.'

He had seen my hesitation.

'I just need some help carrying the heavier stuff, that's all.'

'Okay,' I said, wary.

We left Donald behind for the day. He arranged with the woman across the hall to look in on him from time to time. Then we were in the car and driving. For the first time in our life together, it was me at the wheel. I was sixteen and my driver's licence shone in my pocket.

'Jesus, they wait a long time to give you your licence these days,' he said, beside me in the passenger seat. 'You know I could drive when I was twelve? Drove me mother down to the train so she could get to the camps in New Brunswick.'

I smiled sideways at him, but I was troubled. What was I trying to remember? I hadn't forgotten anything or left anything behind in Sydney Mines. I had my bag with me, I had my driver's licence. I had the sandwiches my grandmother had made for me up at Maryanne and Jessie's.

'You mean you've kept things there all these years?' I asked him, amazed.

'I lived there for a while, you know,' he said.

'The trailer?'

'No. I mean I went back to the *Tïgh Mhór*. I left the trailer as it was. I just kept some stuff in the shed. The trailer,' he said, with a dismissive gesture, 'no, I hardly ever went there.'

We pulled up outside the trailer. I still had that feeling of having forgotten something very important. It was sitting inside my head like an onion, waiting to be unpeeled, layer by layer. Each time I touched it to try to see what it was that I had forgotten, my eyes stung.

We pulled up outside the trailer and got out. I followed him to the steps.

'I'm glad you've come because I need your help with the chainsaw,' he smiled over his shoulder as we mounted the old creaking steps of Grandpa's instant porch, warped and yawed by years of winter.

I nodded. The chainsaw was still in the bathtub. He had kept it there in the trailer too. Sometimes, even in my own distant home I still pull aside shower curtains expecting to see a chainsaw. After eight years, I thought, it must be rusted to the spot.

'Mind the steps.' He looked down. 'I don't think they can support both our weights.'

He put the key in the door. It still fitted. He turned the latch and opened the screen door. It wailed rustily. I don't know why, but I went in behind him.

He peered inside, and tried the light, which still worked.

'What do you know?' The living room and kitchen were illuminated.

It was the smell that hit me. Whole areas of my brain which had been dormant sprang to life again. For the first time in years I felt it slip, the grip I had for so long on my body, its centrifugal, anti-chaotic force. It was the smell that did it.

Inside the trailer it was cold. The kettle was on the stove, where it had sat for eight years. The last cup of tea and the last drop of evaporating water. The quilt was still askew on the sofa where she or I had fallen.

I looked at him.

He shrugged. 'I left that night. I didn't sleep here no more.'

The chainsaw was indeed still in the bathtub. The smell was in here too, combined with enamel and plastic and old chainsaw grease.

It must have smelt like this when they opened Tutankhamun's tomb, I thought. And look what happened to them. Could they feel it, some disease bred in two millennia of stillness, entering their nostrils as they breathed?

'Come down to your old room, Morag,' he called from down the hall.

I ran out of the trailer, and was instantly surrounded by snakes. Grass moved to and fro all around my feet. They were there, buried in the overgrown weed. They were swimming through the grass to come for me. I screamed and hopped over the grass like a kid on a pogo stick, until I stood in relative safety on the highway.

My God, my God. He hung his head in his hands.

The gun clattering to the floor. The second expired.

'Morag!' He yelled.

And then I began to run.

'Morag!' He yelled again, as the porch creaked dangerously beneath him. 'What's wrong?'

But I was off, running up the road. It was half a mile before he caught up to me with the car.

When he pulled up alongside I could see myself reflected in his window. I looked like the fox we had run over that night. There was a kind of terror in my eye.

'What are you looking at me like that for?' He kept pace with me in the car as I ran. He looked in the rear-view mirror to see if anyone was going to come up and plough into the back of him.

I kept on running. He had one hand on the steering wheel.

Was that a rifle he had in his other hand, or only the cigarette lighter?

'Jesus Christ,' he yelled, exasperated. He stopped the car behind me and waited for me to stop. I slowly came to a fast walk, puffing, my heart pounding.

He came up behind me, snatched my arm, whirled me around with his still considerable strength.

'What in the name of Jesus do you think you're doing?' He shouted, his voice hoarse. The car was parked at a crazy angle behind him, tipping over into the ditch.

'What the hell's the matter with you?'

He gripped me tight. The wind off the water hit me in the face.

'There was a dead man following me.' I looked around, confused.

And it was true. This dead man, he had the gun, a big one. A .303. And he carried it under his arm, cocked for firing.

'Are you going queer?' he said, squinting into my eyes for signs of craziness there.

But I knew he was coming to get me now, after failing to finish me off ten years before. He was loading the gun with the moments. His arsenal was full. He had the body of a werewolf and the face of the man. He was the creature that had been waiting in the woods all these years.

'What are you looking at me like that for?'

He was here and now it was all over. The assassin. He asked me: 'Do you know how hard it is to kill someone?'

I said: 'Do you know how easy it is?'

'You could be rotting away in Hell now.' His eyes were ringed with red. His teeth sharp, canine. His gums black, like the gums of Alsatian dogs.

There was a horse galloping down an abandoned railway track, only to find that there was in fact a train coming in the opposite direction, moving across the brown expanse of a November plain.

How many husbands shoot their wives in the middle of nowhere places in Canada and get away with it? There was a hunter in New Brunswick who thought he was shooting a white-tailed deer and shot his wife instead. She had been hanging out the laundry. Big white pillowcases fluttering in the wind, quivering like the tail of a doe. He was drunk. He got diminished responsibility, or some other term that is manufactured by men to let men shoot their wives and get away with it.

The drunken hunter.

'My little doe,' he said, his eyes squinting down the muzzle.

I knew what he was fixing in his sights. He had taught me to shoot after all. He had taught me to fix a woman in his line of vision and to shoot her down.

'She doesn't love you,' he wheezed. 'She just wants protection.'

'I suspected that,' I said now, which was true.

She looked at him hard. Grandma didn't care whether he did it or not. She knew where she was going. And she had always wanted to be a martyr, ever since she was a little girl and had cried at the sadness of it all.

This was the moment that had been coming toward them, all these thirty years of marriage. This moment had woken with them when they woke and had gone to bed when they retired. It was relieved to have been finally set free.

He had come back that night and before she had a chance to say or do anything he saw the gun, leaning gingerly against the kitchen table.

'What's that for?' he asked her.

'I don't know,' she said.

'I'll show you what it's for,' he told her.

I ran over to him as he bent down for the gun and started pummelling his back. He stood up and shook me off as if I were a dog. I landed in the kitchen, near the stove. All I remember was the rage of helplessness, and how it turned my guts to octopi.

The gun was cocked. It was pointed straight at her; it had a monster's mesmerizing gaze, the kind cobras use to paralyse or to lull prey into submission. This was poisonous. Maybe my mother had sent it to them, wrapped in a box.

She looked at him with an unbelievable scorn that said: just do it. Just get it over with and do it, if you're so bent on destruction.

I moved. It was my first conscious real decision. I stood in front of her, right in the line of fire. I stood in front of the gun just as the trigger clicked. He saw me as he heard the release.

I looked into the cyclops eye of the snake, the one out of which would come the little poisonous fang. It was a tunnel, and my life was being sucked backward, toward the beginning. I was a baby in Eden. I was fluttering in my mother's amniotic fluid. My lungs were full and I was drowning on the moment. Someone was spooning an excess of time into my mouth and it was choking me. I heard the click. It was very far away. It was a tiny sound, like the hissing of a snake.

His voice was braying, her voice was shrill, a dog yelping. I had turned to steel, and could not open the door. Where was the person who would save me, whose hand would twist down from the sky and pluck me out?

I could feel claw-like hands on my shoulders. The hands pulled me down. They said, 'Get on the floor.'

The room was hot. I felt very hot and tired, sluggish, all of a sudden. I wanted to lie down and go to sleep. The room was like a sauna, and he held the steaming coals in his hand.

I wanted to show him: this is what you are going to do. I wanted to say: enough of this. You're not going to shoot my mother. You're going to shoot me, whom you profess to love so. And then you'll know what you are.

But it jammed. A second after the gun had failed, he fell to the floor.

My grandfather knelt at the hi-fi, crying into his calloused hands:

'My God, my God, what have I done?'

It sounds like church, I thought.

My God, my God, why hast thou forsaken me?

'Help me, Jesus, sweet Jesus set me free,' he cried.

I could not find with all my soul that I did desire deliverance.

Still kneeling, he wailed: 'Set me free.'

We were caught in this awful stasis in between the chrome and vinyl chairs and the hi-fi.

I had misloaded the gun, the one he had found leaning like an invitation against the table. My hands were small and unpractised, and it was a big gun. So I had the unnatural joy, at eight years old, of having saved or destroyed myself and everyone around me.

Once the moment was over it seemed very far away, like a movie watched out of the wrong end of binoculars. Then it was receding, the moment, taking itself and all that had happened within it and in the years before it away.

That night she and I were on the Trans-Canada Highway to the city and I have been on the same road ever since, driving back and forth, looking for vestiges of the man and the woman and the child and the life they lived together.

TWENTY-SEVEN

T HE Cape Islander boats have been hauled ashore and beached for the winter. Their lime-green fibreglass hulls glint in the slanted winter sun, along with the rusting bridge, the abandoned motels. A trick horse sky at night, pawing the ground, changing colour like slides inserted in a projector then whisked out again. An abandoned child sky by day, its face thin and puckered. I remember the whales we sometimes saw, travelling through the gut, coming up to spray like a distant floating geyser. It's too late in the year for whales now. They have already migrated south.

The tall dark spruce have a startling ferocity, nearly black, standing sentinel, the bayonet thrust of their jaggedness ripping the sky apart. November-thin trees, November-thin sky. The way the light slants from the weak sun as if it is being funnelled through immense venetian blinds. It is as I remember it at this time of year, the landscape. It is a woman pregnant and facing the winter alone: closed, foreboding and obsessed, as ever, with its own density.

I have been very careful with my anger, treating it like a demanding child, with a delicacy rooted in firmness. I will not be too curious. I allow myself few questions, a small number analogous to my supposed indifference.

I know a few things about her. I know she first went to Zimbabwe (then Rhodesia) as a graduate student in sociology, specializing in political responses in emergent Third World cities, with a focus on newly migrated rural populations to urban centres. That's why she spent so much time in Harare and Dar es Salaam. She was a sociologist. She studied other people's realities. She may live there now, in either of those cities, either of those realities. She may have a family there. Or she may live in some small town in Manitoba, teaching sociology in a snowdrift-battered concrete bunker university.

Bridget had lived with them, grown up with them, as I had. He would still have been himself in progress, testing out his strengths, even more violent. I wonder, why did she leave me in a situation she herself had found so intolerable? So that I, her child, would not be spared her complexity?

It was only two weeks ago, a week before he had his accident, when she closed up like a flower. She died that night in the hospital, the yellow light from the parking lot trickling through the venetian blind on her window. He had just been to see her: they saw a little of one another now, he had told me on the telephone, the line obscuring his voice. They were living about thirty miles apart. I hoped she was not afraid when she died. I was still in Australia, unaware of what was taking place on the other side of the world. Visiting hours had finished and everyone had left, thinking they would see her in the morning.

Their funerals will be back-to-back, in different churches. They will be buried in separate graves. Maryanne and Jessie are dead, as is Dan and almost everyone else of their generation. But hundreds of people will be there anyway. They both had the wide acquaintance that is one of the rewards of spending most of your life in more or less one spot. And while people on the island might eschew a wedding or a party in favour of sitting at home with a good cup of strong tea, only the fiercest snowstorm would make them miss a wake. Somehow wakes and funerals are considered much more visceral, more relevant. And the drink was always that much better than the stuff they served at weddings.

This land's face changes with the same fascinating increments of movement as does a lover's face in the act of love. There is endeavour and toil and a furrowed intensity here, and it is not devoid of cruelty.

I stand on almost the same spot where nearly twenty years before Miriam had pointed out the features of our land.

Ta grand'mère ... 'Your grandmother,' she had said. *Quand ta grand'mère était jeune* ... 'When your grandmother was young' ... Miriam said, steel eyes poised on the blue edge of the facing mountain. 'There was none of this hell. She only smiled. People told her she could go to Montréal and be a film star. She looked like Bette Davis, they said. She had a wonderful figure.'

She looked down at me where I stood, eight years old and with my burning palm gripped in her fleshy hand.

Elle était toujours heureuse, she said. *Elle était exactement comme un couteau.*

She was always happy. She was exactly like a knife.

He has left everything to me. I heard from the lawyer by fax. He left virtually nothing to her or to his phantom daughter.

I remember him warning me he was going to do this, years ago.

'I want you to have what you want in life.' He staggered to his feet, and then crumpled like a marionette onto the floor, the unpulled strings splaying around his prone body.

He built me a pedestal of amber, and the late spring sun shone through it, throwing a colour over the freshly melted ground not unlike burning celluloid. I stood onyx and woody on the pedestal, not sure what force had lifted me there.

'I was a boxer, I was a fighter,' he said.

'You were also a welfare-taker and wifebeater,' I reminded him.

193

His face soured. 'Now you're being unfair.'

He is only an actor in this, one of the brutal, black boiled tea-blooded plays about the north: *King Lear* or *Macbeth*. He was the Director, I was the Lead Actress. We shared the take each night, giving a small percentage to my grandmother, otherwise known as The House, so that she could buy us food and clothe us. I got the money. I even got the car, its roof caved in like a sunken soufflé.

I was only the moose, the one that had stepped out in front of his car that autumn. I stepped out and stopped the action. I stopped the play dead. I watched him somersault into the ditch of the orchestra pit. And then I limped away offstage, and kept on going, exhausted for years by what I had done.

We were the three of us nothing more than a highly aware group of actors, hostages to our lines, intelligent enough to know what we were enacting; tryers, I suspect; tenacious people. People who could not let go of reality until they had milked it of all possible incident.

Oh Sir, she smiled no doubt . . .

I gave commands;

Then all smiles stopped together.

I used to quote Browning for him. I was learning the dramatic monologues in high school. I could quote *My Last Duchess* verbatim. He loved to hear it. I always knew as I recited it that I sided with the Duke and not with the supple blameless Duchess.

Because I wanted to be the Duke.

He taught me to want that.

THE TRICKSTER

I saw the photograph in some book, perhaps it was *History of the Plains Indians*. It was so sepia-old it looked as if it had been developed in coffee.

It is 3 January, five days after the massacre at Wounded Knee. Big Foot, the leader of the Ghost Dancers of the Miniconjou Sioux, lies dead in the snow. Five Plains winter nights have embalmed the corpse. His hands are set at the same twisted angle as stroke victims'. A scarf is wrapped around his head. He wears a white man's overcoat. Rigor mortis has set in, practically doubling up his body, so that while Big Foot died lying back on the ground he has now begun to sit up, rising, bent at the stomach, from the snow.

He looks like he is resurrecting himself. He looks like he is reaching for something.

West wind on the Bras d'or lakes, black sky. Thick purples gather at twilight, when the lakes are slaked of an amethyst thirst.

Why do the scrub-grass and the spidery alders turn rust-red in November? As if the colours of the land announced, like prophecy, the coming of the month of blood.

The sky is only power sucked backwards by wind tunnels formed in between the shards of clouds, which are advancing relentlessly toward the sea. This is a wonderfully deranged, savage landscape, the ground breeding a shrill euphoria, like the passion of Gospel singers wailing up into the rafters of a church. The earth breaks away in cracks and fissures as it falls into the sea and the crags and fjords that belong to millions-of-years-old Norwegian rock are formed and re-formed again.

The sky is streaked alternately by green and purple. The gun-metal greys of winter glint against the last phosphorescent blue light climbing down the trunks of birches, gleaming in their pastel hue, the white bark the perfect screen for reflecting the shifting colours of twilight. Around their band of luminescence the sky turns from blue to night.

I stand on the spot where the trailer stood, where it all happened. It is November, almost winter. The month that Chief Dan said was the dying time of year. They are dead, both of them. At the place that was first home there is only a scorched oil tank to mark where the *Tigh Mhór* stood. It is still green with the coat of paint he gave it the last summer we lived there. Around the edges, rust is growing like eczema. The base of the chimney pokes out of the grass where charred pieces of car-bonized wood are still visible. The old foundations of the house have been swallowed up by the grass and the alder trees. Snakes course through the waves of long grass, unencumbered now by the scythe's blade.

Like Ozymandias, I am surrounded by the gutted monuments of self-proclamation: the foundations of houses once grand, the flattened ground upon which the trailer stood, that few square feet where so much happened. I am a traveller in a recently antique land, so I must be detached. I will not, for instance, see my grandfather suddenly spring up from the steep path that leads down to the brook, a bunch of wild roses in his hand, although the roses are long since withered on their stalks.

'Here,' he says, thrusting them at me. 'Throw these on my grave. It's a nice melodramatic gesture. I'm not in it anyway. I'm here. This is my home, as it was yours too.'

And the sun shines in June, and the strawberries grow ripe in the garden while the plums plummet from the thick branches of the tree beside the rose garden.

'Here,' he says, reaching for his hanky. 'Don't get all nostalgic.'

This is the moment, with his emergence over the sharp crest of the hill to the brook, this moment with the still-black-haired man who holds roses in his hand, who ignores the sting of their thorns.

'Here,' he says, stabbing me with pansies. 'Take these for your grandmother. Tell her to find the biggest vase and put them on the kitchen table. It's my birthday today, and I'm going to make her happy.'

This is the moment which is happening forever. It revolves around me, resplendent and cynical in its reality, as I stand in the November desolation, the scrub-brush tickling my ankles, the thickening four o'clock gloom.

It is the hour of the Trickster, the cusp time when Dan said I had to be careful. This is when the Trickster will come with myths in his hands, thrusting them at me, so that I will be obliged to accept them and then to be lost in the continual futility of reinterpretation.

And so the Big House rematerializes in front of me; the newly painted red shutters and the green tank, rustless and verdant, adorn the house. It is filled with the thuds of dancing feet. It is stocked with china and with mahogany and with photographs of my mother. I realize that everything that happened in that house was at once ravishing and sinister and feel the werewolf's sharp nail on my shoulder.

But my grandfather is coming toward me from the brook. He is wearing no shirt; it is a hot day in June, his birthday. He walks by the roses on the path, and their thorns have pierced his flesh. Small beads of blood glisten on the nicks scattered over his chest and his back.

'You look like Christ,' I laugh.

'I am Christ.' He is serious.

And suddenly his neck is loose, his head hanging off his torso at an improbable angle. He is black and stiff. He has two days' stubble on his chin, two days' growth when his hair had continued to grow – when all other functions of his body had shut down – as he lay there, dangling upside down for thirty-six hours.

He revs the engine now, to get the car up the hill. As soon as he takes the turn the car begins to fish-tail. He is going at sixty miles an hour. He shoves his Greek fisherman's cap back further on his head with his thumb and grips the steering wheel, now bucking like a daft calf, with both hands. He lets the cigarette lighter, which was until that second between the index and third finger on his right hand, fall to the floor.

Sonofabitch, he says, and the snowflakes billow into his windshield before being deftly quartered by the wipers.

He went off the highway as neatly as a seal slides off the ice floe into the sea.

Four-thirty in the morning, driving snow and sleet, and he had had too much to drink. No one saw him go over the steep bank, or heard the impact. The silent snow, choking all sound, the bloodless corpse. His harmonica, fallen out of his pocket, on the roof, which is now the floor. His cap, askew over his face.

He does not die right away. Maybe he freezes to death before he is asphyxiated. I wonder if he knows there will not be another night for him. Only this one when the stars are his ground and the ground his sky. No one finds him for nearly two days, when a farmer out fixing his barbed-wire fences sees the car, upside down and nearly hidden by the incline of the bank and by snow.

'Jesus,' I say to him, shaking my head and folding my arms across my chest. We are standing by the *Tigh Mhór*'s old strawberry patch. 'What a fucking mess.'

'Yeah, well,' he shrugs. 'Never mind that. Go with your mother. You can leave me now. It's all right. I won't get angry no more.'

I stand there, stupid with the roses that he has thrust into my hands.

What does he mean, go with my mother?

'Go on,' he waves me away. 'She's waiting for you.'

It is one of the first days in winter, and he is cold. He hangs upside down by straps. Waiting for that light to come arcing over the horizon from Greenland, the arctic promise of a new morning, the bare-boned timber trees, the thick harvest moon and the fields of autumn redberries. Waiting, for the music and the light, while the traffic passes above him.

This was a man. A man, a hot day in June, his birthday and he is wearing no shirt.

A man crucified by roses.